"Are you going to hate me forever?" Luke asked

With more strength than she thought she possessed, Becky pulled her arm away. "I don't hate you."

"Well, it sure feels like it."

"It's just your imagination."

"It's not, Becky, and you know it. It happened so long ago and we were teenagers. Why can't we get beyond that? Why won't you let me explain?"

"Because it doesn't matter anymore."

"It does to me."

The tone of his voice sent ripples of awareness through her. That teenage love had been the strongest she'd ever felt and his betrayal had hurt all the more because of it. "I was seventeen, skinny with freckles and glasses, and Luke Chisum asked me to a dance. My head was in the clouds and I never even wondered why. I should have."

He grimaced. "The first date was a dare. I've admitted that, but those dates afterward were because I wanted to be with you."

Dear Reader,

This is the fifth and final book in the Harlequin Superromance TEXAS HOLD 'EM miniseries. It's not too late to pull up a chair and join the fun. You might learn something about poker—or maybe something more important. After all, everyone needs to know how to bluff, when to fold 'em and when to take a risk and go all in.

In *Texas Bluff*, the hero, Luke Chisum, is known for living on the edge. So when the love of his life, Becky Parker, breaks his heart, he joins the army and leaves River Bluff, Texas. Sixteen years later he receives an honorable medical discharge and returns home to face the past. And to face Becky.

Luke is the type of man who can handle just about anything. I threw some heavy stuff at him, though, and there were times I didn't know if he and Becky would ever find their way back to each other. But I was rooting for them all the way and I'm hoping you will be, too.

Be sure to watch for my next book in June, *Always a Mother*. If you're a mother or have a mother, as we all do, you won't want to miss it.

May you always be a winner, in life and in love.

Linda Warren

P.S. It's always a pleasure to hear from readers. You can e-mail me at Lw1508@aol.com or write me at P.O. Box 5182, Bryan, TX 77805 or visit my Web site at www.lindawarren.net. Your letters will be answered.

TEXAS BLUFF
Linda Warren

HARLEQUIN®

TORONTO • NEW YORK • LONDON
AMSTERDAM • PARIS • SYDNEY • HAMBURG
STOCKHOLM • ATHENS • TOKYO • MILAN • MADRID
PRAGUE • WARSAW • BUDAPEST • AUCKLAND

ISBN-13: 978-0-373-78215-4
ISBN-10:   0-373-78215-2

TEXAS BLUFF

www.eHarlequin.com

Printed in U.S.A.

ABOUT THE AUTHOR

Award-winning, bestselling author Linda Warren has written twenty-one books for Harlequin Super-romance and Harlequin American Romance. She grew up in the farming and ranch-ing community of Smetana, Texas, the only girl in a family of boys. She loves to write about Texas, and from time to time scenes and characters from her childhood show up in her books. Linda lives in College Station, Texas, not far from her birthplace, with her husband, Billy, and a menagerie of wild animals, from Canada geese to bobcats. Visit her Web site at www.lindawarren.net.

Books by Linda Warren

Don't miss any of our special offers. Write to us at the following address for information on our newest releases.

Harlequin Reader Service
U.S.: 3010 Walden Ave., P.O. Box 1325, Buffalo, NY 14269
Canadian: P.O. Box 609, Fort Erie, Ont. L2A 5X3

A special thanks to our nephew Chief Warrant Office 2 Christopher Lee Barnes—United States Army—for so patiently answering my incessant questions about helicopters. Chris is assigned to the 4th Infantry Division in Fort Hood, Texas, and is in training to fly an Apache helicopter. We know that soon he'll be headed for Iraq. Our thoughts and prayers will go with him and with all the young men who sacrifice so much for us.

CHAPTER ONE

To Luke Chisum, coming home was like walking naked down Main Street. He felt exposed. Vulnerable. Everyone in the county knew every misdeed he'd ever done and they never missed a chance to remind him. He'd spent years running from his past, but the moment he stepped foot in River Bluff, Texas, he became daredevil Luke, eighteen, wild and a little crazy.

The last thing he needed first thing this morning was a confrontation with the woman who more than anyone stirred memories of his misspent youth—Rebecca Lynn Parker. But there she was, standing on the sidewalk in front of the medical clinic. With a sigh, he swerved his truck into a parking spot.

The morning sun glistened off her auburn hair, a display of fiery waves and sparkling sunlight. As he reached to turn off the ignition, he was unable to look away. Not from her, not from a long list of regrets and recriminations.

She'd married, and her last name was Howard now. He'd never get used to that. The thought settled in his stomach like a pile of rusty nails. It had been his fault. He'd had his chance with Becky and he'd blown it—big-time.

One of those reminders that followed him everywhere.

Like the scar across his side and the gash on his leg.

He removed his keys, never taking his eyes off her. She barely resembled the young girl from their high school days. Then, her unmanageable curly hair had been usually pulled back into a fuzzy ponytail. She'd worn glasses, had never worn makeup and had a sprinkling of freckles across her nose. She hadn't been beautiful by any means, but she'd had a fresh, innocent appeal that even a foolish boy of eighteen could recognize.

Luke shifted uneasily in his seat.

Even though she was shy and quiet, everyone liked her—including Luke. She'd helped him with his homework more times than he could remember. Being the sheriff's daughter kept her out of the dating scene, though. Sheriff Hubbard Parker got the message across to all the boys—"Mess with my daughter and it's jail or hell, my choice." Everyone knew what jail meant but no one was sure what the hell part meant, and they weren't brave enough to find out.

One night as his high school Texas Hold 'Em poker buddies were playing and drinking, they talked about who they were going to take to an upcoming school dance. Jake, Brady and Cole already had dates. Luke had just broken up with Candace Spangler and decided he wasn't going.

The guys insisted he had to go, but he pointed out that all the girls had been paired up by now. Jake said he could ask Becky. Everyone laughed. Brady looked right at Luke and dared him. They all knew that baiting Luke got results.

Jake double dared him. Cole topped that with a triple dare.

Luke folded out of the round. "Y'all think I won't do it."

Brady called and won the hand. Shuffling the cards, Brady replied, "I don't think even you have enough guts." He dealt the hole cards around the table.

Luke picked up his two cards, not comfortable with his friends thinking he was afraid of the sheriff, even though he was. "I'll ask her."

Cole folded. "Well, Luke, you can be the first one to find out what jail or hell means. Or which comes first."

The guys laughed, but Luke had made up his mind. The next day he asked Becky and she accepted. The night of the dance he stood on the sheriff's front porch thinking he had more guts than common sense. The urge to run was strong.

The sheriff opened the door. He stood over six feet, and was broad and muscular. Luke was tall himself, but Hub Parker seemed like a giant. The gun on his hip reinforced Luke's urge to run. Then Becky came into the room. His fear quickly subsided. Her blue eyes sparkled and her warm smile welcomed him. For the first time he realized she was pretty.

"Good night, Daddy." She stood on tiptoes to kiss her father's cheek.

The sheriff pointed a finger at Luke. "No speeding with my daughter in your truck." The growl in his voice reminded Luke of Mr. Bailey's junkyard dog.

"Yes, sir," Luke replied without taking a breath.

"And, Chisum, you have my daughter home by midnight or I'll come looking for you."

"Yes, sir." Luke backed out of the house knowing hell included a large dose of fear, just as he was experiencing at that moment.

He soon forgot about the sheriff. He kept an eye on his watch most of the night, though, but he and Becky had a good time. They danced, laughed and talked. He didn't do much talking with other girls, and he found he liked talking to Becky.

At eleven they left the dance and went to the Dairy Queen for a burger and fries. Then he took her home. He didn't kiss her because he knew the sheriff was on the other side of the door. But he'd wanted to.

The next Monday in school he couldn't wait to see her. Becky wore a perpetual smile and it was one of the things he liked about her. She was friendly, nice and sweet. That was why everyone called her Sweet Becky Lynn.

He never noticed those qualities in other girls. Hot and sexy were the qualities at the top of his list. A great personality wasn't required of his dates and neither was scintillating conversation. He had been such a puffed-up idiot in high school. But he hadn't been a complete loser—at least he'd recognized all of Becky's good qualities.

They'd started dating and had become an item. The sheriff's place was next to the Chisum ranch, and he and Becky would meet on weekends by the pond on the Chisum property. The first time he kissed her was under the big live oak that hung partially out over the pond. They'd made love for the first time under that tree. Sweet Becky Lynn had taken on a whole new meaning for him.

Luke ran his hand over the steering wheel. How could something that started so perfectly go so wrong? Even as he asked himself the question, he knew the answer. Someone had told Becky about the dare. He was never quite sure who and it was just as well. He would probably have done them some bodily harm.

That time was forever imprinted in his memory. Becky had waited for him after gym class. She hadn't been smiling, her eyes had been red and she'd looked as if she'd been crying. He'd known something was wrong. A heavy feeling had settled in his gut.

When he walked up to her, she held out the chain with his senior ring he'd given her for her birthday.

"You don't have to pretend anymore. I know the truth."

He stared down at the chain and ring in her hand, not making a move to take them. "What are you talking about?"

"You asked me out because your friends dared you. All the kids are laughing behind my back. I can't believe you'd do that. You made a fool of me."

The pain in her eyes was almost more than he could take. He should have told her the truth long ago, but it didn't seem important. They loved each other—that was all that mattered. Or so his young mind had thought.

"Okay. The first date was a dare." She flinched at his admission and he realized he was about to lose something vital to his existence. "But after that I asked you out because I wanted to."

"I don't believe you. I bet you and your poker buddies had fun laughing about gullible Becky, easy, gullible Becky." She threw the chain at his chest and it fell to the concrete. "I don't want to ever see you again." Turning abruptly, she ran to her car.

"Becky," he shouted. As he made to go after her, he stepped on his ring. He bent and picked it up.

Brady, Jake and Cole came out of the gym. They stared at Luke, who was blankly examining the chain in his hand.

"What happened?" Brady asked.

Luke glared at his friends. "Who told her?"

Jake frowned. "What?"

"Someone told Becky about the dare."

Collectively, they took a step backward, shaking their heads in denial.

"Man, that's bad," Cole said.

"Why haven't you told her before now?" Brady asked.

"Shut up." Luke sprinted for his truck, cursing himself for being so stupid. He had to make Becky understand.

When he drove into Becky's yard, he saw her car and knew she was home. The sheriff's patrol car was there, too, but that didn't deter Luke. He had to see Becky.

The sheriff opened the door before Luke reached it, and closed it behind himself. "Go

home, Chisum. You're not welcome here."
The deep growl in his voice would have
frightened a sane person, but not Luke.

"I want to see Becky." He stepped onto
the porch, determined to bypass the sheriff.
The next thing he knew, the sheriff's fist
connected with his jaw like a nine-pound
hammer, sending him flying backward to
the yard. He lay flat on his back staring up
at a blurry sky, the fictional Tweety Bird
circling his dazed head.

That was his first taste of hell.

The sheriff's bulky frame stood over him.
"Stay away from my daughter or I'll kill
you, Chisum. Now get off this property."

Somehow Luke made it home. His jaw
ached for a week, but he never gave up on
seeing Becky. As many times as he tried to
talk to her, though, each time she refused to
listen. He began to see a side of her he didn't
like—her stubborn side. So he said to hell
with her. If she could forget him so easily,
then she didn't really love him.

When she started dating Danny Howard
he thought he'd die, and he knew he had to
get out of River Bluff as soon as he could.

His second taste of hell.

He joined the army and said goodbye to

his family, who were in shock at his sudden decision. He spent sixteen years serving his country, rising to the rank of Chief Warrant Officer 4. He flew a Black Hawk helicopter. His latest mission in Iraq had been rescuing wounded soldiers and flying them to safety and aid. His fellow soldiers called him the Texas Ace because he was from Texas and when he was free for any length of time he was playing poker.

His last rescue had almost killed him. A soldier was down behind enemy lines, and Luke and a medic flew in late at night to retrieve him. On the way back, the copter was detected and insurgents fired at them. Luke knew the Hawk was hit and he fought to control the unstable aircraft. They were losing altitude, and Luke smelled smoke and fuel and knew they were going down fast. Struggling with the controls, he was determined to land the Hawk. He was never quite sure how he did it, but the helicopter bumped hard, skidded on the ground and spun to a stop. He jumped from the cockpit, helped the medic with the now unconscious soldier and the three of them bolted for safety. They made it about twenty yards when the helicopter exploded.

He woke up in a base hospital and was then flown to Walter Reed in Washington. After many tests he was diagnosed with a severe concussion, dislocated shoulder, broken ribs, multiple cuts, burns and bruises. One doctor told him he was one lucky son of a bitch. Although the medic and the other soldier were alive, too, the soldier had lost a foot, the medic an arm.

In the days that followed, the medical team discovered Luke had other complications. He had an inner-ear disturbance and some vision problems. After several weeks, the inner-ear trouble was corrected and his wounds healed, but he had trouble seeing certain colors. His vision had to be perfect for him to fly. The doctor said he'd served his time and recommended an honorable medical discharge.

Luke fought it. He wasn't ready to leave the army or to go home. Then he thought of his father's stroke and knew he was needed at Great Oaks.

In the six months he'd been back, he'd seen Becky several times and she'd always been polite. But when she looked at him, the blue daggers of her eyes could be classified as lethal weapons. He thought they could get beyond what had happened in high school, but he supposed some things just never changed. At least Becky hadn't; she still hated him.

He usually gave her her space.

Today wasn't one of those days.

He climbed out of his truck and headed toward her. She was rummaging in her purse, looking for something. In high school they'd spent a lot of time looking for her glasses, her keys and her books. She was always misplacing things. Seemed that hadn't changed, either.

"Hi, Sweet Bec."

"Morning, Luke." She kept digging in her purse, not sparing him a glance.

"Did you lose something?"

"No. I did not lose anything." She threw the strap over her shoulder, car keys in her hand. "And please don't call me Sweet Bec."

Sweet Bec had been his pet name for her and it had slipped out. Or maybe he just wanted to annoy her. Her eyes met his and Luke thought if looks could kill, he would be dead. He hooked his thumbs into the pockets of his jeans. "Why? Does it make you remember?"

"Don't flatter yourself." Her hand touched her hair, the only sign he made her nervous. The stylish short cut came below her ears and her fuzzy curls had been tamed. He wasn't sure if she'd had them straightened or whatever women did to their hair. The fetching freckles across her nose were no longer visible. Neither were her glasses. Evidently she now wore contacts and makeup.

She looked different, older and definitely more mature. For a moment he was nostalgic for the young Becky who'd constantly pushed her glasses up her nose and who could light up his life with just her smile. He wondered if she'd forgotten how to smile.

Had he been the cause of its demise?

"How are your folks?" she asked when he didn't respond.

He shifted gears to the present. "Fine. My dad is out of his eye drops. The clinic is loaning us some until I can get into San Antonio."

"I told your mom I'd drop them by if she needed me to."

Becky was a nurse and worked in the River Bluff High School. She helped out at the clinic, too. She helped anyone who needed her. That was typical Becky. His mom depended on her advice and that irritated Luke. He wasn't sure why, but in a small town it was hard to keep their lives separate.

"I can take care of my parents." The words came out harsher than he'd intended.

"Mom! Mom!"

A young boy came running toward them. Luke stiffened. He knew who the kid was. He'd seen him around, but he'd never spoken to him and didn't want to now. With the controlled discipline he had learned in the army, he stood ready to meet Becky and Danny's son.

"Shane, what are you doing here?" Becky asked, irritation in her voice. "I told you I'd be at the clinic about an hour and you and Brad were supposed to finish your homework. I was just on my way to pick the two of you up for school."

"Mrs. Grant got a call that her mother had fallen and was in the emergency room in San Antonio. She and Brad left real fast. She wanted to bring me over here, but I told her I'd walk."

"I don't like it when you change plans on me."

"Chill, Mom. It's only two blocks and I'm not six years old. Besides, it was an emergency and I know you wouldn't want Mrs. Grant taking time to drive me to my mommy."

Becky's lips tightened. "No. And don't be smart."

"Ah, Mom." The boy threw his arm across Becky's shoulder and hugged her. "Stop trying to be so tough."

Luke found he was staring at the boy. He had to be about fourteen or fifteen, tall for his age with wavy brown hair and blue eyes. He looked just like Becky, except for the hair. He didn't see a lot of Danny in the kid.

"You're Luke Chisum," Shane said unexpectedly.

"Yes." Luke found his voice.

"Do you think you'll be hiring at the Circle C Ranch for the summer? I'm saving money to buy a truck when I turn sixteen."

"It's just the end of February and I'm not sure yet about the summer, but we're always looking for good cowboys. You'll have to speak to my brother, Hank. He does all the hiring."

Shane grimaced. "He's not too friendly. I already asked and he told me to come back when I was older."

"Shane, you never said you spoke with Hank." Becky frowned, obviously displeased. "Your father's going to help with the truck." She glanced at Luke. "We don't need to discuss this in front of Mr. Chisum. Come on, it's time to get you to school."

"Dad wants to buy me one of those little Ford Rangers. It's like a toy. I want a Chevy Z71 with four-wheel drive, all-terrain tires and—"

"Shane…"

Shane winked at Luke. "My mom's really an angel, but some days you have to search for those wings."

Mother and son got into a silver Tahoe and drove away. Shane waved and Luke waved back. The kid had a great sense of humor. He was Danny Howard's kid, though. Luke couldn't seem to get beyond that. Becky and Danny were divorced, but it didn't keep that seed of jealousy from sprouting in Luke. How could she have married him?

The past hit him smack in the face then. He felt eighteen and angry. Why did life have to be so cruel?

BECKY CLENCHED and unclenched her hands on the steering wheel. She had to mentally calm herself. Every encounter with Luke was the same—emotionally draining. Why did he have to come home? After all these years, she'd thought he was out of her life for good. But she knew he would never be completely out of her heart.

Unable to stop herself, she glanced in the rearview mirror. In jeans, cowboy boots and a Stetson, Luke was unbelievably handsome. He always had been. And the years had added another dimension—one of maturity. His dark hair and eyes were the same, except his eyes weren't as mischievous or flirtatious. They were serious. Luke Chisum was now dead serious. His dare-me arrogance was gone, but his cocky smile showed up now and then—like a few minutes ago.

Does it make you remember?

All the time.

She put it down to first love—the all-consuming love of a teenager. Yet it all had been based on a silly dare. And that dare had sent her self-esteem into the biggest nosedive of her young life.

Luke Chisum could have had any girl he wanted. She should have known there was a reason he'd asked naive Becky to the dance. She'd been so young, and wanted to have fun like the other girls, so she hadn't given it much thought. When a friend had told her the truth, it had broken her heart.

To make matters worse, she'd heard the kids talking. One day after gym class she realized she'd forgotten her purse in her locker. As she hurried back to get it, she heard Bobbie Sue and Stefi, two girls in her class, talking about how gullible Becky was to think Luke really loved her. They went on to say that Luke was just after the sex, all the guys were.

And she noticed the boys glancing at her with pity in their eyes. She just wanted to crawl away and die. All she could think was Luke didn't love her as he'd said. He was in the relationship for the sex. That knowledge almost killed her and led to restless dreams where he was laughing with his friends at just how easy she'd been.

Through the pain, though, she recognized she might be blowing everything out of proportion. The healing process took a long time and when she was finally ready to listen to Luke, he was gone. She wrote several letters, but never mailed any. His leaving reinforced her original beliefs. If

Luke had really loved her, he wouldn't have been so eager to leave River Bluff.

Even though she couldn't get Luke out of her head, she'd plunged headfirst into a relationship with Danny. After a couple of years, they'd known the marriage wasn't working and had gone their separate ways.

But they had Shane.

Becky lived her life for her son. She worked in the River Bluff school system so she could be near Shane. Raising a young boy wasn't easy, especially since Shane was getting older. The thought of him driving was giving her nightmares. Just like his father, he drove like a race-car driver—fast and reckless.

"Luke Chisum's cool," Shane said, pushing the buttons on the radio and twisting in his seat to the beat of Rascal Flatts.

She took a deep breath. "Do not, and I repeat, do not ask the Chisums for a job again. Your grandpa has plenty of work for you to do."

"Mo-o-om," he dragged out her name in a pained tone. "Grandpa pays pennies. The Chisums pay top dollar. If I work all summer, I could buy the coolest truck."

"Shane, did you hear what I just said?" She used her strongest voice, the one Shane knew well.

"Yes, ma'am." He slumped in his seat.

Silence filled the cab.

"Your father called and wants to know if you'd like to come for the weekend."

She heard a muttered, "No."

"You haven't seen your father and his family for two months." Danny had remarried and had two more children. Shane felt left out.

"They live in the city and there's nothing to do there. I always have to babysit. Besides, Grandpa and I are working on the four wheeler. We almost have it running again. Call Dad and tell him I'll come another time."

"You call him tonight and tell him that."

"Mo-o-om." He dragged out her name again in protest.

"You'll call him."

Divorce was hell on kids. Danny understood Shane had a life in River Bluff and didn't pressure him too much to come and visit. Noreen, his wife, had a lot to do with that.

Becky pulled into the parking lot.

"Just think, Mom." Shane unbuckled his seat belt, back to his happy self. He never stayed upset for long. "When I get my truck, you won't have to drive me to school anymore."

Turning off the ignition, she glanced at him. "But remember I'll still be here."

"You know, Mom, those elementary kids need a nurse a lot more than us grown-ups. You might want to think about transferring."

She pinched his cheek. "In your dreams, hotshot."

"Mo-o-om… Oh, there's Abby. Gotta go. See you after school. Remember I have basketball practice." He grabbed his backpack and in a burst of energy was gone.

Becky watched as he joined Abby and more of their friends, flashing his registered-on-the-Richter-scale smile. Her son was handsome, charming and a handful. That caused her many sleepless nights. Shane was like his father in so many ways.

And she was grateful no one saw that but her.

CHAPTER TWO

LUKE SPED DOWN THE ROAD to Great Oaks, the Chisum home. Huge live oaks lined the lane on both sides, their large branches intertwining and creating a canopy effect. The trees had grown on the property long before Luke was born. His great-grandmother had planted them and had named the two-story Victorian house, built by her husband.

Every time he drove beneath the trees, he felt that sense of vulnerability, just as he had in town. He'd been adopted as a newborn by the Chisums and he was always acutely aware he wasn't a blood Chisum. His brother, Hank, made sure he never forgot that little fact.

Hank had been sixteen when Henry and Lucy had decided to adopt. Hank had resented his new brother from day one. Luke was now thirty-four and only tolerated by him, at best. The tension at home had been another reason he'd bolted for freedom, but Hank hadn't been the catalyst that had sent Luke out into the world. Becky had. If Luke hadn't been so eaten up with jealousy over Becky and Danny, he would never have left the Circle C or his parents.

Luke may not have been blood but his roots ran deep with the Chisums. He loved them, even Hank, though it would probably take a bottle of Jack Daniel's to get him to admit that out loud.

Parking at the garages, Luke noticed Hank's Ford King Ranch pickup. He'd been visiting his daughter, Chelsea, in San Antonio. Hank and his wife, Marla, were separated and Chelsea lived with her mother. He hadn't come home the night before so maybe he and Marla were trying to work things out.

Marla was a city girl and hadn't taken to living on a ranch. Luke had been in the military for a year when his mom had written that Marla and Chelsea had moved out for good. Hank had bought them a house and nothing had changed in that situation for fifteen years. Chelsea was now twenty-two, finishing her last year of college. Luke barely knew his niece.

Luke had to give Marla credit. She really tried, but not many people could put up with Hank's moodiness.

Luke slipped out of his truck and took a moment to breathe in the fresh country air. He caught the scent of cypress wafting from the Medina River. Oh, yeah, he was home. Just being here gave him a sense of peace. He'd left here a boy feeling ten feet tall and bulletproof. That was a trick of his young, arrogant mind. He'd seen the world as no eighteen-year-old should—through blood and tears. He'd come back a man with his head squarely on his shoulders, knowing no one was invincible and a bullet showed no discretion.

He glanced in the direction of the barns, corrals, bunkhouse and the rolling hills beyond. Everything lay in the dormant stages of winter. Cedars, spruces and craggy ledges stood out among the bare, weblike branches of the trees. Leaves in different shades of brown blanketed the ground.

Soon spring would turn the landscape into lush hills, green valleys and sunny vistas that were stunning in their simplicity and beauty. To Luke, no place on earth could compete with the scenery in River Bluff. No place.

Cowboys were saddling up for a day on the range. Luke waved to Pee Wee, Newt, Ramrod, Hardy and Paco as they loaded hay onto a flatbed trailer. This was cowboy country. An old-fashioned way of doing things was still alive in the county, even though dude ranches were a common sight around River Bluff. But not at the Circle C. Real tobacco-chewing, bowlegged cowboys worked here.

"Hey, boy, when's the next poker game?" Happenstance Jones, cowboy extraordinaire and ranch foreman, walked from the house, his worn boots making a shuffling noise on the pavement. At seventy-two, Hap wasn't known for picking up his feet.

"Wednesday night."

"Where?"

"Jake's place."

"Might join ya." Hap bobbed his head up and down.

"Be happy to take your money."

Hap snorted, laying a hand on the hood of Luke's truck. "You just gettin' home?"

Luke pushed back his hat. "Hap, those days of staying out all night are gone."

"What are you talkin' about?" Hap spit chewing tobacco on the ground. "You're in your prime. You'd better ride that bull while you can, boy, because before you know it, you'll be ridin' toward eighty like me."

Hap looked every year of his age. He had brown leathery skin from too many hours in the sun. A bony body and bowed legs added to the effect. But Luke knew his mind was still as sharp as the razor the housekeeper, Clover, made him use on the odd occasion. Most of the time he had a gray stubble and a look that was known to frighten small children.

Luke folded his arms across his chest. "Hap, I never thought you worried about age."

"I don't. That's up to the good Lord. I'll die with my boots on and a smile on my face."

"Since I've never seen you smile that might be totally impossible."

"Really?" Hap rubbed his stubble. "I'm smiling now. Can't ya tell?"

Luke studied the strained, wrinkly face. "Nope. Looks more like you have gas."

Hap walked off, shaking his head. "Boy don't know nuthin'."

Luke strolled into the house with a grin on his face. "Hey, Clover."

Clover Jankowski, the housekeeper, turned from the sink and wiped her hands on her apron. With an ample bosom and stout body, Clover had a direct way of speaking that irritated most people. But Luke knew she had a heart of gold once you chiseled through the stony exterior.

If Hap didn't smile, Clover was the reason. In a bad mood, she was known to be as mean as a rattlesnake, and her sharp tongue could be just as deadly.

Luke never understood their relationship. Both came from an orphanage in San Antonio and had started working on the Circle C as teenagers. Hap and Clover always had breakfast together. Trading insults was part of the menu. On Saturday nights they went dancing. Sunday mornings they attended mass together. Whatever their relationship was, it worked for them.

"You get the drops?"

"Yes, ma'am."

"Took you long enough."

Luke kissed her rounded cheek. "Thank you."

"You should've been back thirty minutes ago, and don't think you can sweeten me up with a kiss, young man."

He shook his head. "Clo, I don't think there's enough sugar in the world."

A smile twitched at the corners of her mouth. "Stop foolin' around. Your parents are waitin' for you."

As Luke walked into the den, he heard voices.

"Henry, please eat. You won't get stronger if you don't." That was his mother's concerned voice.

"Stop mothering me, Lu. My eyes burn and I don't feel like eating." His words were only slightly slurred. His speech had improved so much.

"Mom, just let Pa rest for now." Big brother Hank always sided with their father, and it was probably the reason Henry was so stubborn at times. He knew Hank would back him if he didn't want to do something.

Luke took in the scene. His father was sitting in his chair still in his pajamas, a shell of his former self. He'd lost so much weight Luke had hardly recognized him when he'd first returned home. Wan and frail, he was so unlike the strong, hard-nosed patriarch of the Chisum family. It tore at Luke's heart.

Breakfast sat on a TV tray and his mother

wrung her hands in distress. Hank stood over them, trying to look authoritative.

Hank noticed Luke first. "It's about damn time you showed up."

Luke ignored him. "Lean back your head and I'll put the drops in," he said to his father.

Henry complied and Luke administered the required drops. After a moment, Henry sighed. "That's better."

Luke sat on the footstool at Henry's feet. "Good. Now you're going to eat breakfast."

"Son, I'm just not…"

Luke wasn't listening to any objections. He pushed the button on the power chair to raise his father to a sitting position, then placed the tray over his knees.

"Whole-grain cereal with a banana, muffin and fresh fruit. How does that sound?"

"Like sissy food."

Henry favored bacon and eggs with biscuits and gravy. That kind of food wasn't going to be on his menu anytime soon. If ever again.

"You're not going to act like one, though, right?"

"A pissant couldn't eat this crud."

"Pa."

"Ah, okay."

Luke watched as he fumbled with the spoon, wanting to help him so badly. But Henry had to do things for himself.

"When you finish eating, you're getting dressed."

"What for? I'm not going anywhere."

"I want to show you the Black Angus bulls you saved. They've matured and are some mighty fine animals."

"And they'll sire some mighty fine calves." His dad's voice grew excited.

"You bet."

Henry ate a portion of the food then motioned for Luke to move the tray. "Lucy, where's my walker?"

Luke moved the tray out of harm's way as Lucy brought the walker. Henry shuffled toward the hall with Lucy behind him. His mother was becoming so thin. Waiting on Henry was wearing her down. He tried to relieve her of some of her chores, but she always resisted his efforts. He had to try harder.

"The miracle worker, the favorite son has returned," Hank derided.

"Shut up, Hank."

"What are your plans? Are you just gonna sponge off Mom and Pa?"

"Like you?" he fired back without a thought.

Hank bristled just as Luke knew he would. "I work my damn ass off to keep this ranch running. Since Pa's stroke I've had to do everything. You've been no help whatsoever."

He kept his cool. "I'm here to help Mom, and this is my home."

"So that means you have no plans."

Luke stood eye-to-eye with his brother. They were the same height with the same dark hair and eyes. Luke may not have Chisum blood but he was matched perfectly with similar features. He had age on his side, broad shoulders and tight muscles. At fifty, Hank was getting soft around the middle, but what he lacked in muscle he made up for in sheer arrogance.

"I told you I'm here to help Mom. Can't you see how tired she is?"

"She has help. Clover's here and Paco's wife helps out when Mom needs her. In the morning you get your ass in the saddle ready to ride. You'll inherit this ranch and it's time you earned it. Everything's been given to you on a silver platter."

Luke didn't rise to the bait. "You want me to be one of the hired hands?"

"Something wrong with that?"

"Damn right. You're not giving me orders twenty-four hours a day."

Hank scowled. "You're a spoiled rich kid, Luke. You can't handle the work. You can't handle being a cowboy."

Luke got in his face. "If I can handle a war, big brother, I can handle anything you can dish out."

"What's all the shoutin' about?" Clover stood in the doorway. "I got a cast-iron skillet that can stop this arguing, and I'm not afraid to use it."

Hank turned toward the door then swung back. "We're putting a new fence between us and the Parker place. It's been down for some time. Do you think you could dredge up enough energy to ride over and tell the Parkers?"

Several objections popped into his head like red flags, but he didn't voice them. The mere thought of old Sheriff Parker made him feel eighteen and afraid. It wasn't a fear of the man himself. It was that he'd proved the man right. Luke wasn't worthy of his daughter.

"I'm sure the Parkers can figure out what's going on without me telling them."

"Since the fence has been down, Becky's kid rides his all-terrain vehicle on our property. If he doesn't know the fence is up, he'll fly through there and the barbed wire will rip him to shreds. Is that what you want?"

Luke clenched his jaw until his head hurt, but Hank took his silence as an affirmative answer. He'd rather do anything than go over to the Parkers'. Becky lived with her father, so she'd be there. A polite phone call would work just as well. Besides, seeing Becky twice in one day was more than his blood pressure could take.

LUKE KEPT HIS DAD OUT on the ranch, determined he wasn't going to sit in the house all day. They looked at the young bulls and his dad was excited, taking an interest. After lunch, Luke took him to see the paint horses, his dad's pet project.

The horses were kept separate from the cattle operation in their own pasture, corral and barn. Luke stopped the truck, helped his dad out and they walked to the pipe fence.

A brown-and-white stallion threw up his head and stood on his hind legs. "Cochise needs to be ridden," Henry said. "It'll take some of that fire out of him."

Cochise pranced along the fence line. The tobiano paint had a white star on his forehead, and showed a marked degree of refinement and beauty in his strong-boned and well-balanced body. Paints were known for their distinctive coat pattern. Cochise's face, neck, chest, belly and one flank were brown. The rest of his coat was white, including four stocking feet.

Luke hoped he was seeing the beautiful colors correctly, but he still had a problem distinguishing the hues of reds and greens. It was a minor disability compared to what other soldiers had to deal with.

And it was a whole lot better than dying.

Leaning on the fence, he thought it strange that when he looked at Becky, he saw her in brilliant color. Could that be from memory? He quickly brushed the question away.

He glanced at his dad. "I'll ask the doctor when you can start riding again."

Henry grunted. "Not anytime soon. Can barely use my arm and leg."

"That'll improve, just like your speech has."

"Maybe. But I want you to ride Cochise."

"Sure. I'll give him a workout."

His dad grew tired and Luke drove him back to the house. Lucy met them at the door.

"Did you enjoy yourself?" she asked eagerly.

"Don't fuss, Lu." Henry slumped into his chair. "Bring me a cup of coffee."

"I'll get it," Luke said. His dad had a tendency to bellow orders at his mother and it kept her running all day.

When he carried the coffee to him, Henry was asleep. Luke set it on the TV tray.

"He's just worn-out," Lucy said.

"That's good for him."

Lucy suddenly hugged Luke around his waist. A petite woman, her head barely came to his shoulders. "I'm glad you're home. Henry responds to you. Hank makes him so angry."

Luke hugged her back. Except for Becky, he'd missed his mom the most while he'd been away from home. "The past few months have been rough on everyone."

"Yes." Lucy glanced at her husband.

"He's just been so depressed. I was thinking of calling Becky to see if I needed to speak to the doctor about it."

"Mom, you don't have to speak to Becky. Just call the doctor." It irritated him that she depended on Becky for advice.

His mother frowned at him. "What's wrong with talking to Becky?"

"Nothing." He grabbed his hat and swung toward the door. "I gotta go. Dad wants me to ride Cochise."

"You be careful. That horse has a mean streak," Lucy called after him.

Not like some of the enemies he'd faced, he thought as he strolled toward the barn. Enemies who'd hated him and wanted him and his fellow soldiers dead. But his mom didn't need to know that.

Cochise resisted the bridle, prancing around. After calming the horse, Luke saddled up. Cochise flung up his head, standing on his hind legs. Luke was prepared and they shot out of the barn like a rocket. Luke let him run, enjoying the wind on his face and the speed beneath him.

He slowed the horse to a trot as they neared the Parker place. Out of the corner of his eye, he saw a four wheeler fly by. The all-terrain vehicle zoomed over hills and rocky ledges then suddenly flipped, throwing the rider into the winter weeds.

Luke galloped toward the prone boy and swung from the saddle. Becky's son lay completely still. Luke checked the pulse in his neck. There was a steady beat. Thank God.

As Luke took a deep breath, the boy stirred. "Ooooh."

"Don't move, kid," Luke ordered. "Let me check and see if anything's broken." He moved his hands over the boy's body. Nothing seemed broken. Holding Shane's head, he helped him to sit up. "You okay?"

"Oh, man." Shane stared at the four wheeler on its side, smoke billowing from the motor. "Grandpa's gonna beat me black and blue."

Luke frowned. "Does your grandfather hit you?"

"What?" Shane shook his head, still in a daze. "Heck, no. It just… You'd have to know my grandpa to understand. When I've done something wrong, he has a look on his face that makes me wish he'd just hit me. But if anyone touched me, my grandpa would kill them."

Luke knew the feeling very well. Subconsciously he rubbed his jaw where he'd felt the full ire of Sheriff Parker.

Shane stood, brushed dirt from his jeans and sweatshirt then walked over to the wrecked vehicle. "Ah, man. We just fixed it. I guess I'd better go and tell him."

Luke jerked the four wheeler into an upright position and observed the damages. The left front fender was smashed into a tire.

"You just have to fix a fender," Luke told him. "The tire looks okay."

"Yeah, and Grandpa will make me pay for it. At this rate I'll never get a truck."

Luke adjusted his adult thinking hat. "You were going a little fast."

Those blue eyes drilled into him. "You're not gonna lecture me about speed, are you?"

"Would it help?"

"No. You're Luke Chisum. You tried to see if your Mustang would fly."

Luke winced. "You've heard that story?"

"Sure. Everybody in River Bluff has."

"Well, take it from an expert—speed could get you killed."

Luke wondered what the kid would say if he told him his mother was the reason he'd attempted such a thing. After high school graduation, he and his buddies had had a poker party with a keg of beer. Luke had kept drinking to get Becky and Danny out of his mind. He'd lost big that night.

His parents had given him a new Mustang for graduation. Afterward he was bragging to his buddies how fast it could go. He went a step further and told them he could make it fly. They called his bluff. After that there was no stopping him. When his friends realized he was stone drunk and serious, they tried to talk sense into him, to no avail.

The Mustang sailed off a rocky crevice into the Medina River. The river broke his fall, and he had minor cuts and bruises. He spent three days in the hospital and Becky never came to see him. That hurt more than his battered body.

When he was released, he knew he had to leave River Bluff or he was going to kill himself with stupidity. So he'd enlisted, and he often wondered why he felt a need to live life on the edge—in a danger zone.

"I'd better go tell my mom and Grandpa." Shane's words brought him back to the present.

"Come on, kid." Luke grabbed Cochise's reins. "I'll give you a ride."

"On the paint?" Shane's eyes grew big.

"You bet."

"Wow."

Luke swung into the saddle, reached out his hand to Shane and pulled him up behind him. "Hold on." Luke dug in his heels and Cochise sped away.

The horse covered the ground to the Parker place in minutes and Luke braced himself for another confrontation with Becky.

BECKY CAME OUT the back door, looking at her watch. "Dad, have you seen Shane? He needs to start his homework."

Hub Parker glanced up from putting tools away. At seventy, he was still a tall, big man, but his muscles now sagged and his face was etched into a permanent frown. As a child and young girl, she'd done everything to please her father. He'd been bigger than life. Since her mother had died, he'd been the center of her world—until Luke. She'd disappointed her father in a way no girl should, but he'd been there for her when she'd needed him the most.

Hub wiped his hands on a rag. "We got the four wheeler running and he's giving it a spin."

Becky looked to the east. "I hope he's not riding on Chisum land. Hank doesn't like him to frighten the cattle."

"Shane knows better."

The words no sooner left her dad's mouth than they saw the horse and riders.

"Oh, no," slipped from her throat.

Hub touched her shoulder. "Stay calm, girl."

Becky ran to the horse, knowing something was wrong. Shane slid to the ground and she saw his skinned face and hand. "What happened?" Pushing back Shane's hair, she examined his face.

Shane pulled away. "I'm fine, Mom."

"What happened?"

"Now don't have a cow. I wrecked the wheeler."

Fear turned her stomach. "Are you okay?"

He shrugged. "Sure."

Luke stood beside her and a familiar heat emanated from his body. Instinctively she moved away, closer to her son. "Were you riding on Chisum land?"

Shane shifted his feet. "Yeah. Now you can have a cow."

She gritted her teeth and managed to keep her cool. "Go to the house."

"Mo-o-om."

"Go. I'll be there in a minute."

Shane hung his head and slowly made his way to the house. Her father met him.

"Boy, you just never learn."

"I'm sorry, Grandpa."

Shane glanced toward Luke and a look passed between them. What did that mean? Her son didn't even know Luke. Did he? For the first time, Becky felt her parental control slipping.

Shane disappeared inside and her father said, "I'll go get the four wheeler." He headed for his truck.

Taking a breath, she turned and faced Luke. "Thank you for bringing him home. I'll make sure he stays off Chisum property."

He frowned. "Is that a hard, fast rule around here? I remember a time when you rode freely from one property to the other."

Unable to answer, she swung toward the house. Luke caught her arm. *Don't touch me,* her inner voice screamed. Outwardly she stared down at the strong fingers closed around her skin. Fingers she remembered well. Fingers that had stroked, caressed and taught her about love. For months she'd been fighting this very thing, but with just a touch, his touch, the past connected to the present.

And she didn't know what to do.

She raised her eyes to his. The warmth she saw there made her feel as if she were wrapped in brown velvet.

"Are you going to hate me forever?" Luke asked.

With more strength than she thought she possessed, she pulled her arm away. "I don't hate you."

"Well, it sure feels like it. Every time I get within ten feet of you, your eyes are like heat-seeking missiles directed straight at me."

"It's just your imagination."

"It's not, Becky, and you know it. It happened so long ago and we were teenagers. Why can't we get beyond that? Why won't you let me explain?"

"Because it doesn't matter anymore."

"It does to me."

The tone of his voice sent a ripple of

awareness through her and something happened she swore never would—she weakened in her stance to never listen to Luke again. That teenage love had been the strongest she'd ever felt and his betrayal had hurt all the more because of it. But she still wasn't able to let it go.

She looked him square in the eye. "I meant nothing to you. I was a dare. You wanted to prove you could sleep with the sheriff's daughter. It became a challenge for you. I'm sure your poker buddies waited for the news."

"Neither my poker friends nor your father had anything to do with our relationship. That was between you and me. If you can believe such things, then I guess we never had much of anything. I'm tired of beating my head against your stubborn pride. I won't bother you again." In an angry movement, he swung into the saddle. He looked down at her, his eyes as dark as the secret in her soul. "I guess I knew that when I wrecked the Mustang and you never even came to the hospital."

He galloped away, the hooves of the paint kicking up dust.

She wrapped her arms around her waist,

feeling that pain of long ago when she'd heard Luke had sailed his Mustang into the Medina River. She'd waited at the hospital until Henry, Lucy and Hank had left, then she'd slipped into Luke's room. Heavily drugged, he'd been completely out. Her heart had contracted at the bandages on his head, arms and legs. Sitting by his bedside, she'd wondered what she was going to say if he woke up.

But he'd never moved. That morning when he'd begun to stir, she'd quickly left. She'd met Lucy in the hall, but Becky had hurried past her, unable to handle a conversation.

I was there, Luke.

CHAPTER THREE

LUKE RODE COCHISE HARD, his thoughts driving him. How could she believe those things? Had they been in two different relationships? This was it. He was through apologizing to Becky.

When he saw the sheriff checking the four wheeler, Luke pulled up and dismounted. In his present mood, he was ready to take on the sheriff and anyone else who got in his face.

The sheriff beat at the fender with a hammer, trying to pry it away from the tire.

"Need any help?" Luke shocked himself by asking. And his anger subsided as quickly as Becky had ignited it.

The sheriff looked up; his eyebrows knotted together like a frayed rope. "Nope. Just getting the wheeler ready to load." Two ramps were positioned on the bed of his truck.

Luke tied Cochise's reins to a tree limb. "Would you like me to ride it onto the truck?"

From the steely glint of the sheriff's eyes, Luke thought he was going to refuse, but he replied, "Sure. Help yourself."

Luke straddled the wheeler and turned the key. It spit and sputtered then roared to life. He drove it around then guided it up the steep ramps onto the truck. After killing the motor, he jumped to the ground.

"Thanks. I appreciate the help." The sheriff shoved the ramps inside the bed.

"Mr. Parker."

"Hmm?"

"They're installing a new fence through here in a couple of days. You might want to warn Shane."

"Don't worry. The boy won't be riding on Chisum land again."

"That's no problem."

The sheriff slammed shut the tailgate with a deafening boom. Then there was absolute silence. A deer shot out of the mesquite bushes and quickly disappeared. An armadillo rooted in the leaves before scurrying away. A squirrel darted up a tree. From the strong negative vibes coming from the sheriff, a sane man would follow nature and leave, too.

But Luke had something to say. "Sheriff."

"Hmm?"

"I'm sorry I hurt Becky." Since Becky wouldn't listen to him, he thought he'd tell the man whose respect he'd like to have. "Back then I really loved her."

The sheriff removed his hat and scratched his balding head. "Chisum, you hurt my girl and if you're looking for sympathy from me, you're not going to get it. Besides, it happened a long time ago. It's time for both of you to move on."

"Yes, sir." Luke finally believed that.

The sheriff jammed his hat onto his head. "But I'll tell you one thing, Chisum—you hurt my girl again and this time I will kill you."

Luke nodded, believing that, too.

The old truck rattled out of sight and Luke grabbed Cochise's reins. He swung into the saddle, then galloped toward home. Before reaching the big house, he pulled up and breathed in the fresh evening breeze, slightly tinged with the scent of cypress, cow manure and dust.

He was home, but he'd never felt more alone.

LUKE DIDN'T SLEEP MUCH. In the military for so many years, he had never slept soundly. He was hoping that would change once he returned to civilian life. So far it hadn't. He was down early for breakfast.

Hap sat at the table stuffing bacon and eggs into his mouth.

Clover stood at the stove. "You don't need to be playing poker with those young boys. They'll take all your money."

"Don't tell me what to do, woman. We ain't married," Hap replied around a mouthful of food.

Luke poured a cup of coffee and leaned against the counter. "Why haven't you two ever gotten married?"

"Are you kiddin'?" Hap gulped a swallow of coffee.

"Why would I want to marry him?" Clover thumbed in Hap's direction. "He has no manners, tracks dirt into the house and talks with his mouth full. He eats like a pig and has no common sense. I'd kill him within a week."

"Like you're a Wal-Mart bargain. You nag every moment of every hour of every day. If I were married to you, I'd be begging for someone to shoot me."

Clover pointed a spatula at him. "I'll remember that when you want food again."

Without another word, Hap took his plate

to the sink. When he turned around, he pinched Clover on her butt and she swatted him with the spatula.

"I'm serious, Hap. We promised Sister Mary Margaret we'd help with the fund-raiser at the orphanage and you're not losing your money playing poker."

"Don't worry, Clo," Luke said. "He's a pretty good player. He might win some money."

Hap winked, grabbed his hat and moseyed out.

Clover placed her hands on her hips. "Now that's just encouraging him."

Luke took a sip of coffee. "Clo, we don't try to break anyone. We just have fun."

"Hap's too old to have fun."

Luke suppressed a smile as he sat at the table. Hank walked in with his usual scowl, followed by their parents. His dad was dressed. This was a surprise.

Henry plopped into a chair. "I want oatmeal, Lucy."

"Yes, dear." His mother sounded tired. Or maybe just fed up. Luke watched her. Her jeans and shirt hung on her and her blondish-gray hair was combed back. She never took time to fix it anymore.

"Is the heifer sale all set?" Henry asked.

"Yes, Pa," Hank replied. "Everything is set for the first week in April as always."

"You have invitations ready to send to all the buyers?"

"Of course, that's the point of the sale."

"Don't get smart, boy."

"I've been doing this for years and at fifty I think I can handle just about everything on this ranch."

"Now you listen here—" Henry shifted to face Hank. "Lucy, bring me a cup of coffee."

His mother didn't move or say anything.

Henry turned to her. "Lucy, did you hear me?"

Lucy threw a dish towel onto the counter. "Get your own coffee, Henry."

Complete silence followed those words. The only sound was the ticking of the antique grandfather clock in the corner.

Henry recovered first. "What did you say?"

"I said get your own damn coffee. If you can bellow orders without any consideration for me, then you can wait on yourself. Being ill doesn't give you the right to act like a complete ass."

Lucy ran from the room, tears streaming down her face. Luke forced himself to stay in his seat. His father had to go after her, not Luke or Hank.

Henry frowned. "What did she say?"

Before anyone could reply, Clover answered, "She said you're an ass. Rightfully so, too."

Henry pointed a finger at her. "Watch your mouth. You can be gone in a heartbeat."

"Just say the word, Mr. Henry. The nuns would welcome me back—" Clover paused "—in a heartbeat."

Henry stood abruptly; his chair toppled backward to the hardwood floor making a loud banging noise. Luke jumped to his feet, but his dad didn't need any help. He shuffled off to the den.

Hank and Luke stared at each other in bewilderment. Hank tipped his head toward the den. "Go talk to him."

Luke raised an eyebrow. "Isn't that a job for the oldest?"

"You're the favorite, so get in there."

Luke thought of his father's set expression and decided to give him some time. He'd check on his mother first. He had a feeling she needed him more.

As he walked toward the hall, Hank

snapped, "Luke." But Luke didn't pay him any attention.

He stopped short in the doorway to his parents' bedroom. His mother was throwing clothes into a suitcase.

"Mom, what are you doing?"

"I'm leaving." She grabbed more clothes out of a drawer and dumped them into the case. "He can't treat me like this."

His parents argued, but he'd never seen his mother so upset. He caught her by her forearms. "Mom, look at me."

Tear-filled blue eyes looked at him and he felt a catch in his throat. "Pa's been a little hard to deal with since he's had the stroke, but you've been married for over fifty years. You can't just walk out and leave him."

Lucy gripped him around the waist, sobbing into his chest. "I can't take any more. I just can't."

He smoothed her hair, thinking he'd rather take a bullet on the battlefield than listen to his mother cry. "What do you want me to do?"

She hiccuped and pulled away. Wiping at her eyes, she said, "Call Becky."

Becky. He swallowed. "Why?"

"I can talk to Becky."

"You can talk to me."

"Becky's a woman and she understands. Please, Luke."

His mother curled up on the bed in a fetal position. His chest tightened at the sight. Why couldn't she talk to him? Clearly she needed help he couldn't give her. That wasn't easy to accept.

As he charged upstairs to his room to make the call, he kept thinking the bullet would hurt a lot less. Becky answered on the second ring.

"Becky, this is Luke. My mother would like to see you."

There was a noticeable pause, then she asked, "Is something wrong?"

"Yes," was all he could say.

"I'll be right there."

Luke didn't allow himself to think about Becky. They were now strangers, probably what they'd been all along. He'd just been too pigheaded to admit it.

When he reached the den, his dad was sitting in his chair, staring into space. Hank came over to Luke.

"What happened?"

"Mom's leaving."

Hank's eyes narrowed. "You mean going to town?"

"No. I mean she's packing to leave for good."

Hank turned a shade of gray Luke had never seen before. "But don't panic. I talked to her and she's lying down. She wants to talk to Becky."

Hank nodded. "That's good. She talks to Becky a lot."

Luke glanced at their father. "I talked to Mom, now you talk to Pa."

"I got my hands full with this sale." Hank headed for the kitchen. "So make yourself useful."

Luke wanted to shoot him the finger, but that was a younger Luke. The mature Luke walked over to Henry.

He sat on the footstool and remembered all the times he'd sat here as a kid asking a million questions. "Pa, how do birds fly?" "Why are there stars in the sky?" "What's a Big Dipper?" "How do men walk on the moon?" Henry had answered everything and when he hadn't known the answer, he'd made it up. Luke had believed every word, though. There was nothing his father didn't know. There was nothing his father couldn't beat.

Except being incapacitated.

"Pa, you doing okay?"

"I'm not a man anymore."

"Excuse me?" Luke wasn't sure what his father was talking about.

"I knew she'd leave me and it didn't take long."

The doorbell rang, preventing Luke from getting an explanation. Henry wasn't making any sense. His parents had been married forever.

He shifted his train of thought and concentrated on the woman on the other side of the door. He took a moment, then opened it. Becky was in her work clothes—green nurse's scrubs printed with tiny stethoscopes. Her hair bounced around her nape and her eyes were deep with concern.

"I didn't want to bother you," he said, "but my mother insisted."

"It doesn't matter," she said. "Where's Lucy?"

"In her bedroom."

His parents occupied the master bedroom downstairs. Becky followed him into the den and went directly to Henry.

"How are you this morning, Henry?"

"Not good. Lucy's mad at me."

Luke stood in complete shock. His father was talking to Becky.

"What did you do to make her mad?"

Henry shrugged. "Just being me, you know. And that ain't much these days."

"Are you doing your exercises?"

"Sometimes."

Becky rubbed his shoulder. "All the time, Henry. To get better you have to fight it, and I know you're a fighter."

"Have been all my life."

"Good. I'll go talk to Lucy."

Luke paced as he waited. About twenty minutes later, Becky came out. "Did Mom talk to you?" he asked anxiously.

"Yes."

"So what's wrong besides the obvious?"

"Henry's not able to do a lot of the things he used to."

"I know that."

Becky shoved her hands into the pockets of her top. "I don't think you do."

He frowned. "What do you mean?"

"It's sexual."

Luke swung away. "Oh God. I don't need to hear this."

"Grow up, for heaven's sake. They're your parents but they're also husband and wife. Henry's not able to do what he used to and he thinks it matters to Lucy, but it doesn't. He bellows orders at her because in his mind every time she waits on him that means she still cares for him. But a woman can only take so much yelling and insensitivity."

"Oh." Luke finally understood. "How's Mom now?"

"She's soaking in a hot bath. That'll help to relax her. She called Angela Carrick and they're going to San Antonio to get their hair done and to shop. Lucy needs to do something for herself for a change."

"She's going to be out all day?" That didn't come out the way Luke had intended, but he couldn't take the words back.

"Yes, and I know you'll take care of your father."

He raised an eyebrow. "Really? An insensitive clod like me?"

She pushed her bangs from her forehead. "I overreacted last night. I'm sorry about that, and you're right. We need to put the past behind us. We've both moved on."

"Yeah." He held her gaze. "So why are you still so angry?"

She glanced at her watch. "I've got to go. I'm going to be late for work."

"We're going to have that conversation one of these days, Becky," he called to her retreating back.

With her hand on the doorknob, she turned to look at him, her eyes dark. "You might not like my answer."

"I'll take my chances. I'm a gambler."

She nodded and was gone. Luke went to deal with his parents, but he wasn't so angry now. Becky was talking to him.

THE DAY PROVED to be stressful. Henry barked orders at Hank until he was hoarse. Luke couldn't get him to go back to the house to rest and give them all a break. By late afternoon Henry ran out of steam. All day his dad had not once mentioned Lucy's name.

As Luke drove to the house, he saw his mom maneuver her Cadillac into the garage. She got out smiling. Her hair was done in a new style and hung like a bell around her face. Lucy gathered shopping bags out of the car and still Henry didn't say a word.

Luke sensed a blue norther gathering force, and it was fixing to blow through Great Oaks.

Becky's Tahoe stopped behind them. She got out with a long package. Evidently she'd been in contact with his mother during the day. He didn't know whether to feel good about that or not.

Becky helped Lucy with her bags while Luke got his dad's walker from the back of his truck. Silently they made their way into the house. Henry sank into his chair. His mom and Becky continued down the hall. Luke heard voices coming from his mother's room, happy voices. His dad stared at a blank TV screen, not one flicker of emotion on his set face.

Becky came into the den carrying a cane. "Henry, I have something for you."

Henry looked at her and his eyes went wide at the cane. "I talked to your therapist the other day and he felt you were ready for a cane. Want to try it?"

Without one objection, Henry rose and reached for the cane. Luke watched in wonder.

"Try to pick up your left leg," Becky said. "Great. You're doing great."

"I am, aren't I?" Henry asked, slowly making a circle around the room.

"Yes, you are," Becky answered. "And let

me tell you, you look awfully handsome with that cane."

"You think so?"

"Oh, my, yes."

Henry stopped walking and Luke saw a smile on his face, the first one in days. "You are such a liar, Becky Lynn, but you're so sweet I'm going to believe you."

Becky smiled and Luke felt his heart race. "Will you do me a favor, Henry?"

"Anything."

"Apologize to Lucy."

Luke waited for the stubborn attitude to return, but it didn't. Henry nodded and made his way with the cane down the hall to the bedroom.

"Thank you, Becky," Luke said when the door closed. "I don't think he would have done that for Hank or me."

"You're welcome." She glanced at her watch and he was beginning to see she did that when she was nervous. "I've got to run."

"Becky. You don't really believe I'd brag to my friends about what happened between you and me?"

Her eyes caught his, but she didn't say anything.

"I wouldn't. I would never intentionally hurt you."

Those teenage years and all that emotion hung between them. "I know," she murmured. "You put such a dent in my confidence, though, it's hard to remember that."

She walked out the door before he could gather his thoughts, but he felt a whole lot better about the situation than he had last night.

He heard a sound and listened closely. Was his mother giggling? Yes, he heard it again. When his dad had apologized, he must have done it in style. Luke needed to ask for pointers.

Lucy came into the den, all smiles, wearing a beige linen pantsuit. In makeup and high heels, she didn't even resemble the distraught woman of the morning.

"Where's Clover?" she asked.

"In the kitchen, I suppose."

"Tell her that Henry and I are having dinner in our room tonight."

"Oh. Okay. Does this mean you're staying?"

"What?" She shook her head. "Don't be silly, Luke."

She kissed his cheek and Luke knew his

mother was back. That was good in more ways than one. Tonight was the weekly poker game. Now he could leave the house without a guilty conscience. Maybe things would return to normal, or whatever constituted normal in the Chisum house.

Tonight Luke needed to razz and bullshit with his friends—friends he'd known all his life. It was a release for him, just as it had been in high school, to deal with his crazy dysfunctional family.

Today had been a little crazier than most.

BECKY DROVE INTO HER YARD and parked beside Danny's car. He'd picked up Shane from basketball practice. Shane had called and told his father he didn't want to come for the weekend. Danny didn't like it and wanted to talk to Shane in person.

She got out and watched Danny walk toward her. He was a kind, patient man with thinning blond hair and green eyes. After the divorce, they remained good friends. He tried with Shane but they had nothing in common. Shane loved sports and the outdoors. Danny was a CPA, and going to the movies was his favorite pastime. He knew every movie that had ever been made.

His favorites filled a room lined with shelves from top to bottom.

"Did you talk to him?" Becky asked as he reached her.

Danny waved a hand. He did that a lot when he talked. "He says he has to help Hub with the four wheeler. It's just an excuse. He doesn't want to visit us anymore."

"I'm sorry."

"I know he feels left out, but I have two other kids."

"I'll talk to him again."

Danny looked into her eyes. "Luke is back."

A sliver of fear ran up her back and she didn't know why. "Yes."

"How do you feel about that?"

Becky shrugged. "I see him all the time. It's hard."

There was silence for a moment, then Danny said, "It's time, Becky."

She glanced off to the blue sky and the puffy white cotton clouds. Any minute a cloud was going to split open and dump a whole lot of reality on her. More than she was ready to face.

Now or ever.

She chewed on her lip and admitted the

truth. "Since Luke has been back, I've known the time was coming. But I…I…don't think I can."

"Would you like me to…"

"No. I have to do this myself." This was her problem and she wasn't involving Danny in her life again. He had his own family now. She brushed back her hair. "I'm just worried about Shane."

Danny touched her arm with affection. She wondered, as she had so many times in the past, why his touch didn't ignite her senses. But she couldn't fake it. She'd tried and had ended up hurting both of them.

"If you need me, just call."

After Danny left, she walked to her dad's workshop. He was sanding the fender of the wheeler, getting it ready to paint.

"Why isn't Shane helping you?"

Her father looked up, his eyes partially hidden by his cowboy hat. "You've grounded him, remember? Sometimes you're too hard on the boy."

"Like you were never hard on me."

Hub shoved back his hat. "Like it did any good."

Unable to stop it, a tear slipped from her eye. She quickly brushed it away, but another followed. "Everything I do, I do for Shane and it always seems to be wrong."

Hub laid down his sandpaper and took her in his arms. "C'mon, Rebecca. It's not that bad. You're a wonderful mother."

"But I've lied to him," she sobbed into his chest.

Hub lifted her chin. "Then tell him the truth."

"I don't think I can."

"Why not?"

She fought tears and ran her hands up her arms, feeling the goose bumps. "I've taught Shane how to be kind, considerate, loving, caring, giving and forgiving. He knows how to admit when he's wrong and how winning is important but there's no shame in losing. I've taught him to look for a lesson in the bad things that happen. He's never defeated by much of anything. I've taught him to respect others and to respect himself. But will he remember any of that when I tell him Luke Chisum is his biological father?"

CHAPTER FOUR

LUKE GOT OUT OF HIS TRUCK at the Wild Card Saloon for the weekly poker game. His boots made a crunching sound on the crumbling asphalt. He recognized all the vehicles nosed up to the building. Damn! Harold Knutson was here tonight. The man was a bore and he relayed all their chitchat back to his hairdresser wife, who then spread it all over the community. That was the price of living in a small town.

He slipped his keys into his jeans. Ed Falconetti, owner of the Longhorn Café, was here, too. Ed was from New Jersey and still had his northern accent even after many years of being a Texan. He usually brought food, which was a good thing.

Hap's Circle C truck was parked to the side, ready for an early getaway. Since Clover disapproved, Luke was surprised Hap was here. But then Hap had a way of doing his own thing, with or without Clover's approval.

The old Wild Card Saloon, owned by Jake Chandler, crouched on the banks of the Medina River. It had been neglected for years, with rotted wood and broken windows. But now, with Jake's renovation, it was taking shape. Luke noticed the new roof and the rotted wood stripped away. The old, dilapidated honky-tonk was looking better than it ever had. Rachel Diamonte had a lot to do with the transformation.

As an interior designer, Rachel had desperately needed a job to support her young daughter. Jake had been infatuated with the popular, beautiful Rachel in high school. When she'd shown up in River Bluff again, broke and with a baby, Jake, though reluctant at first, had been there for her. The two were headed for the altar, probably real soon.

Luke was happy for them. Because Jake was the son of a bar owner, and a bastard, the kids and the town had been rough on him. He'd grown up in the back room of the Wild Card and he'd hated it. When Jake had been accused of burning down a barn and killing some horses, his life had gotten a whole lot worse. Sheriff Parker had an eye-witness—Rachel. Then Jake left town and no one had heard from him until a few months ago.

Jake had made it big in the dot-com business and had not intended to return, until his uncle Verne had passed away. He'd come back to get rid of the Wild Card, but then his high school buddies had met again and they'd persuaded him to fix up the old place and to stay. Of course, Rachel had more to do with that than his friends. But they were back together playing poker just like when they were teenagers.

"Luke."

He turned to see his friend Cole.

"Hey, Cole," he responded, glancing at the old saloon. "It's looking good." Cole Lawry was now a building contractor and Jake had hired him to do the renovations.

Cole pushed back his Dallas Cowboys ball cap. "Yeah. Since I've gone into business for myself I don't have as much time as I'd like, but it's getting there. Pretty soon I'll need your muscles to hoist some beams."

Luke frowned. "Haven't you heard I'm an injured vet?"

"Yeah, right."

They were both grinning as they walked to the side door.

Cole was the quiet one of the group. His dad had committed suicide when Cole was young and growing up had been hard for him, too. The friends had played poker as a way to escape their rotten lives. Cole had never strayed from his roots farther than San Antonio. He'd gone though a bad divorce, but he'd found happiness with a newcomer to River Bluff, Tessa Jamison, a woman who'd come to town to find out if Cole was the father of her sister's baby. They still laughed about that. Cole was also the responsible one. He and Tessa were now living together and putting the finishing touches on Cole's house. They were very secretive about their wedding plans.

His friend Brady Carrick had a tug-of-war relationship with his dad, who was always pushing him to excel. And Brady had. He'd played for the Dallas Cowboys and had a stellar career until he'd busted up his knee. After a failed marriage and a stint of playing poker in Vegas—much to his dad's disapproval—Brady was back in River Bluff proving he had what it took to

train a winning horse at his dad's Thoroughbred training facility, Cross Fox Ranch.

Brady was deeply in love with Molly
Davis, a waitress he'd taught to play poker.
She'd even made it to the U.S. Poker Play-
Offs Quarter Finals in Vegas, thanks to
Brady's tutoring. They'd all gone to watch
the event. Molly was now working in the
office at Cross Fox, and living there, too, but
there was no word of a wedding yet. Luke
knew it was only a matter of time.

A new friend, Cole's brother-in-law,
Blake, had joined the group. Blake had been
in prison in a foreign country for a number
of years, and he and Luke connected on a
level that only the two of them could understand.

Blake and Annie were already married
and expecting their first child. The Not So
Wild Bunch, as Annie had named them,
were becoming the Family Bunch.

All except Luke.

He was the loner.

Shoving his hand into his pocket, he ran
his thumb over the raised surface of his dog
tags. He never played poker without them.
His time in Iraq would forever be embla-
zoned in his brain, in his heart and in his

soul. The wild Luke had grown up fast. He'd become responsible, dedicated and loyal. Men had depended on him for their safety.

For their very lives.

But through the hell, bad conditions, lost lives and the horrors of war, he'd never forgotten Becky. The pain of hurting her had never lessened.

Neither had the pain of losing her.

Now he just wanted to make it right.

The responsible Luke had to make it right.

Becky was talking to him without the anger. That was a big step forward. It had taken six months to break through her defenses. Not that he'd actually broken through, but he felt there was a crack now where before there had been a solid wall.

"Luke, Cole," Brady said when they stepped into the back room they used for their games. The small space was still shabby and run-down, but the guys didn't mind. An old battered oak table with scratches and notches took pride of place. That was all they needed. And beer.

He spoke to his friends and looked at Hap, Harold, Ed and Ron, Cole's ex-boss. "You old-timers ready to play?"

Blake glanced at his watch. "I don't want to play too long. Annie's at her mom's having dinner."

"Tessa's there, too," Cole said, "and so are Molly, Rachel and Becky. You don't have to hurry. They'll be talking into the wee hours." Cole grabbed beers out of the old clunker refrigerator and passed them around. "Rachel's giving Tessa some decorating tips on the house. I told her whatever she wants is fine with me."

"You're such a sap." Harold took a swig of his beer. "Stand up like a man and tell her how it's going to be."

Brady laughed. "Yeah. Like you do with Sally." Sally was known to lead Harold around by the nose.

"That's what I'm telling you young guys. Set the rules now or in thirty years she'll be chewing on your ass every night like one of Hap's old hound dogs."

Hap looked up. "Knut, my hounds wouldn't touch your ass."

A round of laughter followed.

Blake opened the silver box with the cards and chips. "Harold, I hope I never have a marriage like yours. Wait—" he held up a hand "—I know I'll never have a marriage like yours. I go to sleep every night with my hand on Annie's stomach. In the morning our child wakes me by kicking against my hand. It's an awesome feeling and I know that's never going to change. The feeling, I mean, not the pregnancy."

Jake pulled out a chair. "I never thought I could get so wrapped up in a child. Never really thought I was father material. But Becky's giving Rachel more exercises for Zoë and we will do them religiously. Rachel and I are going to make sure she has the best life possible."

If anyone was wilder than Luke, it was Jake with his leather jacket and motorcycle. For him to make such a statement about Rachel's Down syndrome baby was a revelation in itself.

"Man, I can relate to that." Brady popped the top on his beer. "I didn't think I could love another man's kid so much, but Sammy feels like my own. Of course, I'm pretty crazy about his mom, too."

All his friends had found their soul mates and Luke wondered if he'd be the only one in limbo. The only one unable to move forward.

He wasn't sure he was still in love with

Becky. But he knew without a doubt that to move forward he had to put the past behind him. So far he'd been unable to do so. That was his struggle and it drove him every day.

"I hope you guys don't mind," Harold said, plopping into a chair, "but I invited someone to join us."

Jake shuffled the cards. "We're not partial to whose money we take, are we, boys?"

"Nah," Cole replied, taking a seat. "Who is it?"

"Guy does my taxes. You boys probably know him."

"Who—" Before the rest of the sentence left Luke's throat, the door opened and Danny Howard stood there. Becky's ex, and the last person Luke wanted to see or have at the poker table.

The room became painfully quiet. Luke could actually hear the gush of the Medina River outside. Or was it the rush of blood in his veins?

Four pairs of eyes stared at him, waiting for his reaction.

He and Brady were the only two standing. Brady leaned over and whispered, "What do you want to do?"

"Nothing," he whispered back, and

walked over to Danny and held out his hand. "Hi, Danny, I don't believe I've seen you since high school."

Since you stole my girl. Since you made my life a living hell.

"Yeah. It's been a long time, Luke." Danny gestured toward the table. "Hope you don't mind my stopping by."

"Of course not. This is River Bluff and all friends are welcome."

You low-down bastard.

Luke passed by Brady on his way to a chair. "Stay cool," Brady murmured under his breath.

Jake's eyes caught his, as did Cole's, both saying the same thing. He wasn't sure what his friends thought he was going to do. Evidently they thought he was as wild and crazy as he ever was. But there was something about being shot out of the air like a clay pigeon that changed a man forever. Of course, he used jokes and ribbing to hide those scars.

But he was mature enough to handle a game of poker with Danny Howard. Now he had to prove it.

"Tournament play, no limit and a fifty-dollar buy in, boys," Jake said. "Let's see some money."

Each player slapped money onto the table and collected their chips.

Jake, the host, gathered the cards and shuffled them, dealing each player two hole cards. The betting started to Jake's left and they settled in to play Texas Hold 'Em. After a round of betting, Hap and Ron were left playing the hand.

Hap called Ron's bet.

Jake laid three cards, the flop, face up on the table.

Studying the cards, Ron made a thumping sound with his chips on the table. After a moment he placed a bet.

Hap raised it.

"Call," Ron said.

Jake dealt the fourth card, the turn card.

Hap took his time, twirling a chip between his fingers. He had the perfect poker face, no emotion whatsoever. Suddenly he mucked his cards.

"Hot damn," Ron yelled. "I knew you didn't have a damn thing." He guzzled his beer.

The evening wore on, with a lot of cursing and a lot of yelling, mostly from Ron. The man could not hold his liquor and by the fourth hand he was out. As were Harold, Cole and Hap.

Jake shuffled the next hand and dealt the hole cards. By the end of the betting, it was Danny, Ed and Brady in the hand.

"Are you just in town to help with Harold's taxes?" Ed asked, frowning at his cards. Ed did not have a poker face.

"No. I came for a visit with my son," Danny replied. "I watched his basketball practice. That boy is really good."

"He's really good with the girls, too." Ed raised Brady's bet. "My granddaughter's nuts about him"

"Becky and I talked about that." Danny raised Ed's bet. "The girls throw themselves at him, but Becky and I warned him about using more discretion when dealing with lovesick girls."

Becky and I. Becky and I. Becky and I.

Luke's stomach clenched so tight he was sure it was wrapped around his backbone. He dug in his pocket for his dog tags and slapped them on the table.

"You're making small talk, Ed, so that means you have squat." Brady stacked one chip on top of another, repeatedly.

"No discussing the bets," Harold snapped.

"Why is it so hard for you guys to follow the rules?"

"Because we love yanking your chain," Brady replied.

"Bastard," Harold muttered and grabbed a hamburger out of a bag Ed had brought.

Ed folded, but Danny won on the river card.

By the end of the evening, three players were left in the game—Luke, Jake and Danny. Chips clicking and the sputter of the old refrigerator were the only sounds in the room.

The next hand Jake studied the cards on the table, his thumb and forefinger caressing a stone from the river he always carried when he played. Luke knew he was serious. Jake went all in and Luke won the hand with three deuces.

That left Luke and Danny in a head-to-head for the top spot. Luke felt that was symbolic. He'd bluff with his last breath before he'd let Danny win. Once in a lifetime was enough, he decided.

Jake dealt the hole cards. Luke had a two of diamonds and a nine of hearts. He had shit. But he threw a chip on the table.

After a few minutes, Danny raised the bet.

Luke raised again and knew he was digging himself a hole.

Danny played with his cards, placing one over the other. He looked at them one more time, his face expressionless, and called.

Luke would have bet that Danny was a fish, an amateur, but he was changing his mind. Luke pulled his hat low and waited, no expression on his face.

Jake laid the flop on the table; queen of clubs, king of spades and a seven of hearts.

Damn! A good poker player knew when to fold. This was it. But something in Luke wouldn't allow him to do that. He placed a bet and dug his hole a little deeper.

Danny raised.

Luke pulled his hat lower and called.

Jake dealt the turn card, a nine of clubs.

Hot damn, now he had something—a pair of nines. But what did Danny have? His face showed nothing. And in that mathematical brain of his, Luke knew Danny had something.

Luke placed a bet.

Sweat popped out on Danny's forehead, the first sign of nervousness. Suddenly he pushed his chips toward the center of the table. "I'm all in."

Luke took a moment and knew there was no way in hell he'd fold. He called.

Chairs squeaked as everyone gathered round.

Danny turned over his hole cards—a pair of tens.

Goddammit!

Luke did the same.

A low rumble of voices followed.

Now they waited for the river card. Luke stood, keeping his eyes on the table and praying for a nine.

Suddenly the room became quiet as they waited for Jake to deal the fifth card. He was taking his time and Luke could feel his friend's eyes on him.

"Get it over with," Luke finally said. "I'm getting older by the minute." He joked to let the guys know he was fine.

But he held his breath as Jake burned a card, and let it out when Jake flipped over the nine of spades.

Danny pushed back his chair. "You're a lucky man, Luke."

Luke noticed that Danny's blond hair was thinning and his green eyes looked worried. In that instant, Luke knew he and Danny were not enemies. They'd just loved the same girl. Danny had won that round because of Luke's stupidity.

He'd always liked Danny in high school. He'd been a smart, affable kid and Luke wondered what had happened in his and Becky's marriage. Why hadn't they stayed together for the sake of their son?

Danny stood. "I'm glad you made it home safe, Luke."

"Thanks. I just have a little color-vision problem." He leaned closer, feeling the tension of the night leaving him. "To tell you the truth, I have X-ray vision at times. You see, I saw the river card was a nine."

Danny's eyes went wide in disbelief.

"Don't believe him," Jake said. "Actually we all look pea-green to him, and that's okay because Luke doesn't know the difference."

Danny smiled. "Still the same old Luke."

"Some things never change." Brady gathered the chips off the table.

"It was good to see you, Danny," Cole added, helping Brady.

Jake divvied up the winnings.

"Maybe I'll catch another game when I'm in town."

"Sure." Luke was counting the seconds in his head, hoping Danny would leave. The small talk was getting to him. He and Danny weren't enemies, but spending his poker night with him wasn't on Luke's list of favorite things to do.

Harold and Ed headed for the door. "See you guys next week," Harold called.

Hap reached for his hat. "See you at the ranch, boy. Remember you're supposed to help round up those calves tomorrow. The rest of you, well, I'll see you when I see you and hopefully not before."

Brady looked up. "Hap, it would be nice if we could decipher what you mean half the time."

"Ah, boys. Now that'd be no fun at all." Hap shuffled toward the door.

"I've got to go, too," Danny said.

As the door closed behind Danny, Blake asked, "Are you okay, Luke?"

"Yep." Luke helped gather the beer cans and trash. "There's something cathartic about facing your past."

"We're adults now and we have to get beyond the high school years. Rachel and I managed it and so can you and Becky. And Danny." Jake placed the cards in the box.

Luke slapped him on the back. "The ever-wise Jake."

"I'm serious, Luke. You and Becky are hung up on that stupid dare. We were teenagers being teenagers. And Rachel is so sorry she ever told Becky."

Luke whirled around. "What did you say?"

Everyone paused as the full implication of those words sank in.

"Rachel told Becky?" The question was like the crack of a whip and everyone seemed frozen in place from the sting.

"Luke…"

But Luke wasn't listening to anything Jake had to say. With one yank, he opened the door and ran for his truck. He revved up the engine, backed out taking three inches of River Bluff dirt with him.

LUKE DROVE STRAIGHT to June Lawry's house, white-knuckling the steering wheel the whole way. *Rachel was the one who told Becky* kept running through his head. Why would she do that? Why would she do that to Becky?

And to him?

He turned into the driveway and jumped out. In a few strides he was at the front door, pounding on it with his fist.

June opened the door. "Luke," she said in surprise. "Is something wrong?"

Through the open doorway he saw Molly, Tessa, Rachel, Annie and Becky sitting in the living room drinking something out of cups. They all stared at him with worried expressions. Reality hit him then. What was he doing? The eighteen-year-old Luke had surfaced without him even realizing it.

Until now.

He removed his hat. "I'm sorry to disturb you, Mrs. Lawry, but may I please speak to Rachel?"

Mrs. Lawry frowned. "You want to speak to Rachel?"

Understandably, June was confused. Even though Luke's temper had cooled, he still had to talk to Rachel. Somehow it was important to him.

Rachel came to the door. "Luke, what is it?"

"Could I speak to you out here, please?" he said.

Rachel briefly glanced back at Becky then stepped outside, closing the door behind her. "What's this about, Luke?"

He gripped his hat, feeling the smoothness of the felt. "Why did you tell Becky about the dare in high school?"

"Oh, Luke, I am sorry. I was a different person back then, consumed with my own world. I never even thought of what it would do to Becky." She brushed back her blond hair. "Kyle and I had an argument and I was crying in the bathroom when Becky found me. I was telling her what jerks guys were. She said you weren't. For some selfish reason, I felt the need to enlighten her. The moment I saw her face, I knew it was wrong, but I couldn't take back the words."

"I see. I wondered all these years who'd told her." He placed his hat on his head. "Now I know."

"Please don't hate me."

He didn't. Because he could clearly see who was at fault. For years he'd blamed the person who'd told Becky. But Rachel wasn't to blame. "I don't hate you, Rachel. If I had told her the truth, I would have saved us a lot of misery. But the truth is very elusive to a teenage boy."

"Luke…"

Rachel was interrupted by four vehicles pulling up to the curb. Jake was the first to barrel out, sprinting to the porch. He looked from Rachel to Luke, his eyes wary.

Luke nodded and strolled down the steps into the cool night air. He met Cole, Brady and Blake, but he kept walking.

"Luke," Brady called.

He raised a hand. "Talk to you later."

Reaching his truck, he realized he'd left his door open. He took a moment to get his head straight.

"Luke."

He whirled around to face Becky.

"WHAT ARE YOU DOING?" Becky asked, wondering what he'd said to Rachel.

Luke shrugged and leaned against the side of his truck. "Just being Luke."

"Why do you keep doing this? Why is it so important to you?"

"I don't know, Bec." He crossed his arms over his chest. "When I was going down in the Hawk, I was pretty sure death was knocking at my door. I had these flashes of my life in my head and most every other frame was your face. My one thought as the chopper hit the ground was I'm going to die and Becky will never know how sorry I am for all the hurt I caused her."

Becky swallowed and wrapped her arms around her waist against the chill of the cool night breeze. But it wasn't the night that sent the chill through her. It was his words. For sixteen years she'd been avoiding this conversation. Now she had to face it.

"Luke, we have to move on." A part of her was still resisting that intrusion into her emotions.

"That's what I'm trying to do." He crossed one booted ankle over the other. "But to put the past behind me, I have to know that you forgive me for being a stupid teenage boy."

She bit her trembling lip.

"Sixteen years is a long time, but what we had back then was powerful and real. I'm the one who screwed up. I take the blame and I'm not angry at Rachel or you. I just want to move forward with my own life."

Oh God, she felt like bawling, and she didn't know why. Maybe it was fear. Maybe it was the thought of finally saying goodbye to their teenage romance. Because that was exactly what she had to do.

For both of them.

"I forgive you, Luke." The words came from deep within her heart where they'd been buried for so many years.

He didn't say anything, but she felt his eyes on her and she rushed into speech. "I'm sorry it took me so long to say that. Back then I was every boy's friend. I helped with their homework, loaned them paper, pens and notebooks. I was the first one they called to find out if so-and-so was interested in them. Not once did any of them ask me to go for a burger or to the movies. I know a lot of that had to do with my father."

"It had everything to do with your father."

"I know, and then Luke Chisum asked me out. I couldn't believe it and I never stopped to ask why. I was so excited because I'd had a crush on you since eighth grade."

"Really?"

"Yeah. And when I found out the truth, I was devastated. I couldn't get beyond all that pain and humiliation."

"Bec…"

"It's okay, Luke. I finally understand what happened. I was just hurt too deeply to listen. I believe teenagers feel things more deeply."

"I'm sorry I hurt you."

"And I'm sorry it took me so long to get to this point. But I'm truly over the past."

He straightened and touched the backs of his fingers to her cheek. "Thanks, Becky. That's all I needed to hear."

Her cheek burned from his touch, and soft lingering memories floated around her. She was glad the darkness hid the expression in her eyes.

"Goodbye, Becky," he said, sliding a long leg into his truck.

"'Night, Luke." For some reason, she couldn't say goodbye. Maybe because she'd said goodbye to Luke a long time ago.

She turned and headed back to the house. *Coward. Coward,* echoed in her head. She hadn't told Luke everything. And she should have.

Annie met her. "Are you okay?"

"Yes. I'm fine," she lied to her best friend.

"Then why are you crying?"

Becky quickly brushed away tears, not even realizing the treacherous waterworks had started.

"I don't believe you're over Luke, like you keep saying." Annie wrapped an arm around her and it was comforting.

"Yes. I'm over Luke." She sniffed and glanced back to see his truck driving away. "It's finally over."

CHAPTER FIVE

LUKE HAD TROUBLE SLEEPING. As soon as he dozed off, the dream returned, as it had so many nights. He could feel the wobble of the Hawk, smell the fuel, hear the soldier's moan and the scream of the medic: "Luke, do something! We're going down!"

He had to control the chopper. Hold on. Steady. Steady. The Hawk kept going down, down, down into a black hole. The blackest hole he'd ever seen.

The hole of death.

His body trembled, but his hands were like steel as he refused to lose control. The bump came then. An earth-shattering crash that spun them farther into the dark hole.

"Luke? Luke!"

He jerked straight up in bed, shaking and soaked with sweat. The past fell away and he realized he was in his bed at Great Oaks, breathing hard and waiting for his heart rate to return to normal.

He swung his legs over the side of the bed, then stood and walked to the window. He pulled back the curtain and stared into the inky darkness. From the floodlights he could see the garages and barns beyond. He was home.

Safe.

Then why did he have the dream?

Becky had forgiven him, so he should be happy. He should be content and at peace with the past and looking forward to the future. Why wasn't he? Why was he still fighting the war inside himself?

He flopped onto the bed, his eyes on the window, waiting for daybreak. Waiting for the light to chase away his shadows— waiting for all those deep, buried feelings for Becky to disappear.

LUKE MUST HAVE DOZED OFF. When he awoke, a dim yellow haze could be seen through the window. He crawled out of bed, showered and dressed, feeling better. And ready to face the day and the future. Now he knew he could without any guilty feelings.

Within minutes he was in the kitchen

sniffing the tantalizing aroma of homemade biscuits. He kissed Clover's cheek. "I'll get the honey."

"It's already on the table."

Luke noticed the oatmeal-colored honey pot with its wooden spoon. The stoneware pot had bluebonnets hand painted on the side. He remembered its spot on the table beside the butter, just as it had been when he was a kid. It had belonged to one of his great-grandparents. Luke couldn't remember which one.

As he poured a cup of coffee, he thought how they weren't really his great-grandparents. He wasn't actually a Chisum.

He never thought too much about his biological parents. For whatever reason, they had given him away and he didn't feel he owed them a lot of space in his head. Lucy and Henry had told him they'd picked him out at an agency. With his similar hair and eye color to Henry, they knew they'd found their second son.

Life wasn't bad.

Except for Hank, who was like a burr under his saddle blanket.

As a teenager, he'd had a problem dealing with Hank's controlling, manipulative, jealous behavior. Now Luke tolerated him with an ease that came with maturity. He knew there were worse things in this world than his brother's bad attitude.

Luke reached into his jeans and pulled out his winnings from the poker game. He laid it on the counter in front of Clover.

"Give that to Sister Mary Margaret. It'll buy a lot of shoes and clothes."

Clover glanced from the money to his face. "You're a sweet boy, Luke."

Before Luke could respond, Hank walked in and poured a cup of coffee. "Where are Mom and Pa?"

Luke looked at the ancient wrought-iron clock on the kitchen wall. "It's not even six. I guess they're still in bed."

"Mom's always up at this hour." Hank took a seat at the table, pulled papers out of his shirt pocket and sorted through them.

Luke didn't respond to the statement because Hank was already on another channel.

"Luke, can you run an errand for me today?"

He straddled a chair, sipping on coffee. "Depends."

"On what?"

"On how nicely you ask me."

Hank's eyes narrowed. "I don't have time for your mouth this morning. Clover, where's the newspaper?" He didn't pause for a breath.

"Then I don't have time, period," Luke responded.

Clover set breakfast and the newspaper in front of Hank. Slipping a plate in front of Luke, she pinched his ear. "Be nice. We help out around here."

"Yes, ma'am." Luke swallowed back a curse word and said, "What do you need me to do?"

"Pick up supplies at the feed store."

"I thought you wanted me to help with the roundup."

"I do. I want the helicopter in the air by ten, but I also need those supplies and I don't have a cowhand to spare." Hank stuffed scrambled eggs into his mouth.

"You should have been a sergeant in the army. Giving orders comes so natural." Luke dribbled honey over his biscuit, deciding he wasn't ready for combat this early in the morning. "Do you have a list?"

"I phoned it in to Scully at the feed store. You just have to take the flatbed trailer and pick it up and be back here by ten."

"Sure. No problem." Luke licked honey from his fingers.

Hank studied him. "You're in a better mood than usual."

"Yep." Luke took a swig of coffee. "I had a nice talk with Becky."

"God, are you still mooning over that girl?"

Luke stiffened at Hank's tone. "That's none of your business."

Hank plopped his napkin on the table. "You know, Luke, you've put Becky on a pedestal like she's a saint or something."

"She is a saint," Luke snapped back.

"Really?" Hank lifted an eyebrow. "This same girl who married Danny Howard while you were still in boot camp and had his child faster than you could say 'Luke who?'"

Luke's chair scraped against the hardwood floor as he sprang to his feet with fire in his eyes. "You talk about her like she's a slut."

"I'm just telling it like it is."

"You—"

Clover slammed a cast-iron skillet onto the table. It sounded like a bomb going off. Hank flinched and Luke jumped back.

"Eat your breakfast before I hurt both of you," Clover said.

Luke eased back into his chair, wondering how Clover could control grown men with just her voice and an empty threat.

"Don't get me wrong, Luke," Hank said, pushing his plate away. "I like Becky. Everyone does. But there was more than one person in that relationship and it's time you stopped taking all the blame."

"Damn, Hank, that's about the nicest thing you've ever said to me."

"Get over it and get your ass to the feed store by seven." Hank rose, grabbed his paper and headed for the door.

"He's a barrel of laughs." Luke carried his plate to the sink.

"Humph," was Clover's reply.

"Hap's late this morning," he commented on his way to the door.

"He's been gone an hour." Clover glanced up from putting dishes in the dishwasher. "It's roundup time and Hap's first in the saddle, some cowboying nonsense."

"Yep. That's Hap."

"Luke."

He turned back.

"Thanks for the money."

He winked and walked out.

BECKY PLACED SHANE'S OATMEAL on the table and shouted, "Shane, hurry up. We have to leave in fifteen minutes."

Shane stumbled into the kitchen in his pajama bottoms, hair hanging in his eyes. "What's the rush?" He yawned and stretched.

Becky pointed to the door. "Go shower and change this instant." Evidently he'd just crawled out of bed and she'd called him thirty minutes ago.

"Mo-o-om."

"Shane, I have to be at the clinic in forty-five minutes to check the schedule and make sure someone is there. If you're not in the car in—"

"Okay. Okay. Jeez."

Becky took a deep breath, trying to control her temper.

"He's just a teenage boy, Rebecca," her father said from behind his paper.

She sat down and reached for her coffee. "You're very lenient in your old age. When I was a kid and you told me to get up, I got up."

Hub laid down his paper. "Your grandmother usually said those words."

"Yeah." She cradled her cup. "I still miss

her." Her grandmother had been strict and stern, but Becky had always felt safe and loved. Becky's mom had passed away when she was two, so Maureen Parker was the only mother she'd ever known. She'd died when Becky had been in high school, and she often thought that if her grandmother had lived she wouldn't have made so many bad choices.

"Mmm." Hub refilled his cup. "Lighten up on the boy. You've gotten a little paranoid since the Katie Hollister incident."

Becky still got chills when she thought about it. She and Annie had seen Shane kissing the girl, who was three years older, then Annie had seen him climbing out of Katie's window one night—a night when he was supposed to be at home in bed.

Danny had had the sex talk with Shane years ago, but she'd found she'd also had to have that talk with him. She wanted to trust him and she wanted him to be honest. He'd told her Katie was in love with Devin and Devin had broken up with her. Shane had agreed to help make Devin jealous and he was flattered by the older girl's attention.

Shane had said they hadn't had sex. Katie had wanted Devin to see Shane crawling in and out of her window. Becky didn't know whether to believe that or not, so she'd given him the safe-sex speech. His face had turned red and he'd said he'd be embarrassed to buy condoms.

She believed him and she didn't even want to think about him having sex without one. Not after what had happened to her. But how did she explain that to a son whose hormones were on the joyride of their life?

"I just want to trust him," she said when she realized her dad was waiting for a response.

"Then do." Hub eased into his chair. "Don't you think I knew where you were going when you said you just wanted to go for a walk?"

Her eyes opened wide. "You knew I was meeting Luke?"

"Pretty much. But I trusted you."

Oh God. At that moment she felt as low as one could get. She'd broken that trust.

"I'm sorry, Dad," was all she could say.

"For what? For falling in love? For being human?"

It felt surreal to talk to her father about this. At the time, she'd been afraid to tell him anything—so afraid of his anger and disappointment.

"For lying to you."

He shrugged. "Teenagers do that. All we can do is be here for Shane, offer advice and guidance. If he screws up, we're still gonna be here, but we can't watch his every move. We have to trust him to be responsible."

Why was I ever afraid of this man? Maybe it hadn't been fear. She'd just been scared of disappointing him. She was his little girl.

She got up and wrapped her arms around his neck. "I love you, Daddy."

Shane breezed in and wolfed down his oatmeal and milk. She was going to warm the oatmeal but he didn't seem to notice it was cold.

"Grandpa," he said in between swallows. "The other day I was over at Wally's car lot and he has this used Chevy dually that's cool. It's bright red and has all this chrome on it. And the wheels are mega heavy duty. I could drive across the low parts of the Medina River without a problem."

"Why would you want to drive across the Medina River?" Becky asked before she could stop herself.

Shane spared her a glance. "To get to the other side. Jeez."

"Well, excuse me. I just assumed that's why we have bridges."

"Girls don't get it, do they Grandpa?"

Hub grinned and stood for another refill.

"Let's go, hotshot," Becky said, her arms encircling his neck. "I love you."

"Jeez, Mom, don't say that out loud anywhere."

She sighed. "I'll be very careful."

As Shane rose from his seat, Becky realized how tall he was getting. He towered over her, mostly arms and legs, but he was filling out, too, becoming a man. Her heart ached for the little boy she was losing.

DRIVING INTO TOWN, the trailer clanging behind his Chevy truck, Luke thought about what Hank had said about Becky. She *had* fallen for Danny rather quickly. Luke had always thought that she'd gone out with Danny to get back at him. Was it more?

And what did it matter? He'd spent too much of his time dwelling on that relationship. He'd traveled the world, had other women, but something about coming home opened up that old wound and all his feelings about Becky.

He turned and drove down Main Street.

Becky was outside the clinic talking to a lady. Her son was chatting with a very pretty blonde.

He waved and Becky waved back. He didn't feel the need to stop and force her to talk to him. They would now be... He thought for a minute. What the hell would they be? Old friends? Old lovers? Maybe just old.

Some days he felt old beyond his years, but as long as he could keep smiling, keep joking, he was going to make it. He had a lot of living to catch up on.

He backed the trailer to the loading dock at the feed store. Scully gave him the thumbs-up sign, and workers started loading feed and supplies onto the trailer.

A car backed in beside him and a bleached blonde got out and climbed the steps to the loading platform. She looked familiar.

He slid out of the truck. "Bobbie Sue Beecham." Bobbie Sue was an old girlfriend from high school—before Becky.

She looked at him, her face splitting into a smile. "Well, I'll be damned if it ain't Luke Chisum. I heard you were back."

He swung onto the platform and she gave him a big hug coated in sinus-clogging perfume. "Now aren't you a sight for sore eyes." She gave him the once-over. "I heard you were awarded the Purple Heart or something."

"You know me, always flying somewhere I shouldn't."

"You devil." She slapped his shoulder. "I remember that time you flew your Mustang into the Medina River. Sure thought you were a goner then."

He rocked back on his heels. "Me, too."

"By the way, the name is Carver now."

He lifted an eyebrow. "You married Willie Carver?"

"The third time." She laughed. "Our divorce was final last month. And I'm trying to make a living working at Sally's Beauty Shop."

"Never left River Bluff, huh?"

"For about five years with husband number one. But I must have steel in my butt because River Bluff is like a magnet always dragging me back."

A young feed-store employee barely out of his teens walked up to her. "Bobbie Sue, your dog food is all loaded."

"Thank you, Jimmy." She smiled at him and he blushed.

Bobbie Sue still had it.

Touching a red-tipped fingernail to Luke's cheek, she said, "Give me a call, handsome, and we'll remember old times." She sashayed down the platform steps in high heels and capri pants. All the guys watched. So did Luke.

He jammed his hands into the pockets of his jeans. Life was looking better. He might take her up on her offer. But then, just as quickly, he knew he wouldn't.

Wild and crazy wasn't something he wanted to be anymore.

Bobbie Sue was definitely wild and crazy.

Damn. He must be old.

The roar of a Harley motor caught his attention. Jake pulled into Bobbie Sue's spot and killed the engine. He removed his helmet and hooked it on the handlebars. Swinging one leg over, he dismounted and adjusted the kickstand.

"Hey, Luke," he said, vaulting onto the platform.

"Jake, what are you doing here?"

"I saw your truck from the road and wanted to make sure everything was okay."

He frowned. "Why wouldn't it be?"

"You were upset last night." Jake ran a

hand through his hair. "I thought you knew Rachel had told Becky."

"No. It came as a bit of a shock, but I'm okay with the whole thing. Like you said, it's time to get beyond the high school years."

Jake looked straight at him. "Do you think you can?"

"You bet." And he'd never felt surer of that. "I was just talking to Bobbie Sue."

"I thought I saw her leave. You're not thinking of taking up with her, are you?"

Luke grinned. "I'm keeping my options open."

"Yeah, right." Jake jumped down. "See you Wednesday." He revved up the motorcycle and was gone.

Luke felt a moment of sadness for those teenage years. For everything that was so urgent, so here-and-now-and-must-be-experienced-today feeling. When in reality an eternity stretched before him.

And he felt no urgency at all.

That was more than sad.

It was growing up.

CHAPTER SIX

LUKE WAS BACK AT THE RANCH by nine. His parents were eating a late breakfast and it was good to see them both in better spirits.

Hank barked orders at him for a solid hour. He was used to orders and took them all in stride, but he was glad to crawl into the cockpit and shut out Hank's voice. Hank had hired a mechanic to maintain the chopper, but Luke checked out the aircraft as he'd been trained to do.

He strapped himself in and put on his headset. Starting the engine, he watched the gauges and followed familiar steps until the aircraft spooled up to one hundred percent hover power. He was ready to go.

When he'd first come home, he hadn't thought he'd ever fly again. Then he'd seen the Bell 206 helicopter Hank had bought for the ranch and the new hangar to house it. At first, he'd been angry, refusing to fly the bird. He hadn't wanted a token gift, but then he'd seen Hank flying it to herd cattle out of thick, wooded, brushy areas, places cowboys couldn't go without danger to the horses. It was a cost-effective machine for a ranch this size. Still, he hadn't been sure about flying. He hadn't since the crash.

But last Christmas, Tessa had been stranded at the airport in San Antonio. The poker guys had decided Luke could fly in, pick up Tessa and deliver her to Cole, who'd thought Tessa was back in Oregon. He hadn't told the guys he'd had that moment of doubt. If he had, they wouldn't have let him in the cockpit.

No way was he letting fear stop him from helping Tessa get to Cole. With Brady as his copilot, and Jake and Blake as his wingmen, they'd taken to the skies. They'd done a little finagling at the airport for a landing spot, but there was nothing the four of them couldn't do. Tessa and Cole had spent Christmas together.

And Luke was flying again.

He just might tell them about that fear one of these days, just to see the look on their faces.

Then again, maybe not.

The big bird soon took to the air and Luke felt at ease and in control. Flying always gave him that feeling. He left the house and buildings behind, heading for the deep southeast of the Circle C. Big brother's orders were to frighten the cattle into the open so the cowboys could herd them across Cypress Creek to the long fenced lanes that led to the corral. From there the cowboys would separate the calves from their mamas and load the calves onto two eighteen-wheel cattle carriers to be hauled to the feed lots.

Luke flew low over the pasture several times. He got close enough to fan the treetops, and the cattle began to scatter into the clearing. The cowboys quickly gathered them into a herd and started the drive toward Cypress Creek.

He could see Hank and Hap waving arms and shouting. Luke could imagine Hank's voice clearly in his head over the hum of the copter.

Suddenly he saw the black cloud—an early spring shower, for sure. Dammit. If they were lucky, maybe the cowboys could get the cattle across Cypress Creek before the rain started.

Their luck didn't hold. Rain splattered against his windshield.

Damn!

He'd have to take the copter back to the hangar.

From his perch above, he could see Hank and Hap riding wildly, shouting orders to the cowboys. He knew the order without hearing it. "Get the cattle across the creek fast." It was known to rise quickly in a rainstorm.

Lightning zigzagged across the sky, spooking the cows. They stampeded toward the creek, jumping into the water in their haste to outrun the lightning and the big bird hovering above them. Luke knew Hank had everything under control. He had to get the copter out of the weather before it worsened.

Suddenly another bolt of lightning zipped through the sky. Luke turned toward home. As he did, he saw Hank's horse rear up and Hank tumble into the creek. His head bobbed up and down as the current took him downstream. Hap was busy with the cattle and didn't notice.

No one did.

Without a second thought, Luke set the copter down and jumped out. After quickly removing his boots, he dove into the chilly water, hoping Hank hadn't made it this far. He swam against the current, searching for Hank as rain beat down on his head, blocking his vision.

For the first time he realized how important perfect eyesight was for combat. Damn. He couldn't miss seeing Hank.

He swam harder.

Then he saw him.

Hank was facedown in the muddy creek water.

Luke swam with all his strength toward his brother. He grabbed him under his armpits and flipped him, trying to get Hank's head out of the water. He was unconscious.

Or was he dead?

Luke blocked that thought as he held Hank and tried to swim toward the bank. The wind was against him and he struggled. But he wouldn't give up. Just like when the Hawk had been going down. Nothing would allow him to give up.

Nothing.

But he could feel the current pulling them down, down, down.

Luke kept fighting to reach the bank, but his legs and arms grew tired. How much longer could he keep them above water?

Out of the corner of his eye, he saw something. Then he felt the rope as it landed over them. Hap was on the bank. Luke made sure the rope was securely around him and Hank, and shouted, "Okay."

The wind took the word, but Hap heard it. He kneed his horse, and the rope tightened and pulled them to safety.

On the muddy ground, Luke disentangled from the rope and bent over Hank. He was cold, blue and not breathing. Chills popped up on Luke's wet skin but he stayed focused.

Hap knelt beside him. "Is he…?"

"No," Luke shouted and began to do CPR. He tilted Hank's head back and listened for breathing. Nothing. He pinched Hank's nose and covered his mouth with his own and blew into his throat. One. Two. Hank's chest rose from Luke's air, but he still wasn't breathing.

Hank lay pale and still.

A fierce determination settled over Luke.

He folded one hand over the other and began chest compressions. Faster and faster he pumped. "Come on, Hank. Come on. Breathe."

Nothing.

"Dammit, Hank. Don't you die on me!" Rain pelted his head and ran down his face; mud soaked through his clothes and chills racked his body, but all he felt was the pain—the pain of losing his brother.

He repeated CPR and began to pound on Hank's chest with driven intensity. "Come on, Hank. Shout at me. Come on. I dare you. Dammit. Breathe!"

"Luke…"

"Shut up, Hap. He's not dead. Breathe, Hank. Breathe."

The rain slowed and several cowboys gathered around, but Luke kept working. Suddenly Hank's chest moved, then he coughed and up came the water. Luke let out a tired breath and quickly turned Hank so he could vomit the putrid stuff.

Luke sucked air into his starved lungs.

"What…the…hell," Hank moaned, his voice hoarse, and Luke thought it was the most beautiful sound he'd ever heard.

Luke struggled to his feet, wiping water from his face. "Help me get him in the helicopter. I'm taking him back to the ranch."

Within minutes, Paco and Newt had Hank inside, and Luke slipped into his position at the controls.

"Tell him not to worry about the cattle," Hap shouted above the roar of the blades. "I'll take care of everything."

Luke nodded and motioned them away from the aircraft. Once he was in the air, he said, "I'm taking you to a hospital in San Antonio."

"Goddammit, just get me to the ranch. Do you… hear…me?"

"Loud and clear, but you need medical attention."

"I'm…fine," Hank groaned, lying flat on the floor.

"Yeah. You look fine and dandy."

"Luke…"

The rain splattered against his windshield and he had a problem seeing. Focus. The ranch was due north. With this visibility he knew he couldn't make it to San Antonio and he probably couldn't get a landing clearance, either.

"You're in luck," he told Hank. "I can't make it in this weather, but I'm calling Becky to check you over."

"Whatever."

Since Luke knew Becky wasn't at the clinic on a Thursday, he poked out her cell number. This was a natural solution. He needed help and Becky could help him. He didn't feel those pains in his stomach the way he usually did.

"Yes." Becky came on the line.

"Could you meet me at the ranch? Hank's had an accident."

"What happened?"

"I think he drowned for a bit, but he's breathing now."

"I'll be right there."

"Nonsense," Hank groaned.

As he landed at the hangar, the rain became a drizzle. He noticed Becky speeding down the road toward him. He turned off the machine and opened the door. Becky climbed in and knelt by Hank, taking his vitals.

"Don't need a damn nurse," Hank mumbled.

Becky ignored him. "His pulse is low and so is his breathing. How long was he in the water?"

"Maybe twenty minutes."

She poked a gadget in Hank's ear. "His temperature is ninety-five point five degrees. We have to get him to a hospital."

"Like hell," Hank said

"You've been deprived of oxygen and the

hospital can check your blood-gas level. You could go into cardiopulmonary arrest. It's only a precaution—a necessary precaution."

"Luke, get this woman…away from me…and get me to the house. Now!"

Luke shrugged and Becky shook her head.

"God, you're stubborn," Becky snapped. "We have to get you comfortable and warm."

Between the two of them, they managed to get Hank into Becky's Tahoe and then into the house. Lucy and Clover were in the kitchen, preparing dinner. Lucy glanced up from the stove.

"OhmyGod! What happened?"

Luke had forgotten how bad they looked, wet, muddy and bedraggled. "It's okay, Mom," he was quick to reassure her. "Hank took a nosedive into Cypress Creek and he liked it so much he decided to drink a gallon or two."

"Funny," Hank muttered. But Luke felt Hank's weight on him. He was as weak as a kitten.

"We have to get him out of these wet clothes immediately," Becky said.

Clover appeared with two bathrobes. Luke wasn't sure Hank could undress himself. He reached for a chair with one hand, while holding Hank with the other, and dragged it and Hank into the large utility room. "We'll be right back," he said to the group as he closed the door.

Hank collapsed into the chair and Luke pulled off Hank's boots. Water spilled everywhere. "Damn, Hank. You have a gallon in your boots. No wonder you were so heavy."

"Son of a bitch, my best…working boots."

"Not anymore." Luke took off Hank's soggy socks and wet shirt. "Stand up so we can remove your jeans and shorts." Hank complied, but almost toppled forward. Luke steadied him, undid his belt and tugged his jeans and shorts over his hips. Hank slumped into the chair and Luke jerked off the jeans.

Hank grabbed the robe, slipped his arms into the sleeves and covered himself, evidently uncomfortable being naked.

"Damn, Hank. I never knew you were prudish."

"Shut up and get me to my room."

"Give me a sec. I have to get out of my wet things." He shimmied out of his clothes in half the time it had taken Hank, then helped him into the den.

Henry walked from the hallway with his cane. "What the…"

"They're fine, honey," Lucy told him. "Hank took a tumble into Cypress Creek."

"Why is Luke wet?"

"Someone had to fish him out," Luke answered.

"You okay, son?"

Neither Luke nor Hank knew who the question was directed at, so neither answered. Finally Luke said, "Hank's fine. He just needs to get some rest."

"I really think you need to go to the emergency room in San Antonio and be checked over by a doctor." Becky spoke to Hank.

"Would you give it a rest? I don't…need a doctor. Luke, get me to my room." A near-death experience hadn't changed Hank's disposition.

It took all of Luke's strength to help him up the stairs and into his room. Once there, Luke thought Hank could use a shower to get the mud off him, but rest was what he needed most. And a new attitude.

Luke helped him to his king-size bed. As he slid beneath the covers, Hank's teeth rattled so loudly that Luke could hear them.

"I'm freezing," Hank mumbled.

A knock at the door prevented Luke from answering. "Come in," he called.

Becky walked in. "How is he?" Then she saw Hank shivering in the bed. "Get more blankets," she said to Luke. "This is what I feared. He has hypothermia." She immediately checked his temperature. "It's below ninety-five now."

They covered Hank with more blankets. Becky looked at Luke. "He needs to go to the hospital."

"Hank, did you hear that?"

"Go…away."

Luke motioned Becky out of the room. "Keep an eye on him. I'm going to call his wife. Sometimes she can get him to do things no one else can. Sometimes."

He hurried to his room and called Marla. She was very agreeable and said she was on her way. But Luke wasn't sure anyone could handle Hank. He'd rather die than admit he needed help.

The mud on Luke's body began to dry and harden. It was uncomfortable and itchy.

Since he was in his room, he decided to take a quick shower. He slipped into jeans and grabbed a shirt, suddenly realizing his boots were on the bank of Cypress Creek. Damn. He'd just bought them when he'd returned home.

Becky poked her head around the door. "Luke, oh, I didn't realize you were dressing."

"You've seen me half-naked before. Hell, you've seen me naked before."

A slight stain colored her cheeks from either embarrassment or anger. Luke wasn't sure so he quickly buttoned his shirt.

She stepped farther into the room. "Do you ever stop joking?"

"Sometimes I can be dead serious, but that wasn't a joke. It was fact."

Her eyes drilled into him. "And you get some perverse pleasure out of reminding me?"

He realized he was stepping over the line once again. "I'm sorry. That was rude."

She brushed back her hair, which was curling around her face from the dampness. "Do you think we're always going to do this to each other?"

"I hope not." He sat in a chair to slip on

a pair of moccasin house shoes. Shoving one foot into soft fur, he asked, "How's Hank?"

"Stubborn. Did you get his wife?"

"She's on her way."

"Maybe she can talk some sense into him." Becky couldn't stop herself from watching Luke. Jeans molded to his long, lean legs. His damp dark hair curled into the collar of his chambray shirt. The sharp bone structure of his face was all angles with a sexy five o'clock shadow. His broad shoulders filled out his shirt. He oozed sex appeal. He wasn't even aware of it. But she was.

That hadn't changed.

Her reaction to it had. She could now control it.

Or could she?

She had an irresistible urge to kiss him—to plant a big smacker on those unforgettable lips, with their tongues dancing, trading saliva, the whole nine yards. To get lost in something basic and primitive and not think. Just feel and enjoy his masculine touch on her soft skin once again.

She had no idea where that feeling came from. It wasn't foreign to her. It was almost necessary to her existence. How could that be? She'd gotten over Luke years ago. She'd learned to live without him.

Then why was she standing here wanting to kiss him so badly that she could actually feel the pain of not doing so?

She shifted from one foot to the other, needing a distraction, needing to regain control. "Why don't Hank and Marla live together?"

He glanced up, his eyes as dark and deep as the desire in her belly. It took every ounce of strength she had not to move forward and touch him.

He stood. "No one but my parents can put up with Hank for any length of time. He's like a cornered bobcat. He comes out fighting all the time, every time."

"Why do you think he feels cornered?"

He shrugged. "Got me. Hank is Hank. I've learned to live with him. And Marla has in her own way. He spends just about every weekend in San Antonio with her and Chelsea."

She stared down at her sneakers. "I guess some people just weren't meant to be together."

"I suppose," he murmured, and their eyes met. Sixteen years hung between them.

Sixteen years of emotions, needs and heart-ache. She wished she could say the words she needed to say, but she couldn't.

The time wasn't right.

She turned toward the door. "I'd better check on Hank."

Would the time ever be right?

CHAPTER SEVEN

THEY MET LUCY IN THE HALL. "Come quick," she cried. "I'm worried about Hank."

Becky charged into the room. Hank was trembling severely in the bed, thrashing about, his teeth chattering. After taking Hank's vitals again, Becky reached for the phone. "I'm calling for an ambulance like I should have from the start."

As her hand touched the phone, the blare of a siren echoed in the distance.

"I think Marla has arrived," Luke said. "I'll open the front door."

He took the stairs two at a time and reached the door just as the ambulance pulled into the driveway, Marla's Mercedes in front of it. She slid out of the car and hurried to the door, motioning to the paramedics.

Tall, slim and blond, Marla was the personification of a sophisticated, beautiful woman. In her younger days, she'd modeled for catalogs and clothing stores. Then she'd married Hank and settled down to raise a family. Sadly, they'd only had Chelsea, and Marla had become completely involved in her daughter's life as well as numerous charitable organizations.

Marla and Hank were so different; Luke had never understood their relationship. They argued constantly. Marla didn't want to live with Henry and Lucy. She wanted her own home, but Hank had balked every time they'd discussed building a house. That Luke really didn't understand. Why did Hank want to continue living with his parents?

In the end, Marla had moved out with their daughter and Luke knew Marla was waiting for Hank to join them. In all these years, it hadn't happened. Hank continued to live at Great Oaks and Marla maintained a residence in San Antonio. They'd never divorced, but stayed married living apart.

What kept Hank tied to Great Oaks?

What kept him from having a normal life with his family?

Even as Luke asked himself the question, he knew the answer. The inheritance— Circle C Ranch. Hank had made it known on more than one occasion that he felt the ranch was his because he was the only biological son. Hank was staying put to make sure Henry didn't give Luke more than he deserved.

It was no secret Luke was the favorite son and that weighed heavily on Hank's mind. Someday soon he and Hank would have to talk about it.

"Where is he?" Marla asked, brushing past Luke in a platinum linen pantsuit, heels and a whiff of expensive perfume.

"In his room," Luke replied, opening the front door wider to allow the paramedics inside with a stretcher.

He followed them upstairs.

The paramedics quickly loaded Hank, strapping him down. Becky rattled off medical information as they rolled Hank toward the door.

"Lu-ke," Hank called weakly.

"I'm right here, brother." Luke moved to the stretcher.

"I need…to tell…you…" His teeth chattered between each word.

"Save it, Hank." Marla patted Hank's shoulder. "You can thank Luke later."

"Hey, babe," Hank said as he heard her voice.

"We have to go." Marla motioned to the paramedics.

They wheeled Hank out the door. "Lu-ke. Lu-ke. Lu-ke," Hank kept calling as they took him away.

Luke wasn't sure what Hank was trying to say. Was his brother delirious?

In a matter of minutes, they had Hank in the ambulance. Marla climbed inside, too. "I'll leave my car here."

"Don't worry," Luke told her. "I'll get it to you."

With the siren blaring, the ambulance tore away.

"Do you think he'll be okay?" Lucy asked, her voice cracking.

Luke put his arm around her. "Sure, Mom. Hank's tough. Anyone else would have died on the banks of Cypress Creek."

"Don't joke, son," Lucy scolded. "I'm going to change my clothes and we're going to the hospital."

"Yes, ma'am."

His mother went inside and Becky glanced at her watch. "I've got to run or I'll be late picking up Shane."

He looked into her blue eyes. "Thanks, Bec. I appreciate all of your help today."

"No problem. Friends help friends." She didn't look at him.

"So we're friends now?"

"We've always been friends." She looked at him then and he felt that barrier she kept between them—like an invisible solid wall of steel.

"Yeah," he replied with less enthusiasm than he'd intended. He swiped a hand through his hair. "I apologize for barging in last night at Mrs. Lawry's. I just lost it when I found out Rachel had been the one to tell you about the dare."

"It's okay, Luke. It made me realize how childish I was being."

Before Luke could respond, Lucy shouted from the house, "Luke, let's go."

They hurried inside. Becky said goodbye and quickly left. Luke ran upstairs for a pair of boots and soon he was driving Marla's Mercedes to San Antonio with his parents following him.

They would now be friends, he kept thinking.

That was much better than the cold shoulder. A part of him wondered why there couldn't be more. But he knew. Becky's for-giveness wasn't complete.

She still didn't trust him.

BECKY WAS LATE. Most of the kids had been picked up. A couple lingered outside, but Shane wasn't in sight. She got out and asked one of the boys, "Where's Shane?"

The boy thumbed toward the gym with a smirk on his face.

Becky pushed opened the steel door and went inside. She paused for a moment as she spotted her son. Shane propped himself against a wall and Brittany Dunbar, a cheer-leader and a junior, leaned into him, her breast pressing into his side.

Get away from my son. She-devil.

Shane made no effort to move away. Nor did Becky expect him to.

He was male and a teenager.

She took a long breath and remembered she had to trust her son.

"Shane," she called in her sweetest voice.

He immediately straightened. "Mom." Guilt flashed across his face like a neon sign.

"Hi, Mrs. Howard." Brittany lifted a hand.

"Brittany."

Trollop.

"I'm sorry I'm late. Are you ready?"

"Sure." Shane grabbed his backpack from the floor.

"Brittany, do you need a lift?" Becky forced herself to ask. As a mother, she couldn't leave the girl here alone.

"Thanks, but my mom is, like, you know, talking to the coach."

"Oh." Becky had forgotten that Brittany's mom dated the basketball coach.

"Bye, Shane," Brittany called. Her voice was thick and sweet like blackstrap molasses and Becky gritted her teeth at the syrupy sound.

"See you tomorrow," Shane said as they walked out.

Her son was the proverbial fly strip, attracting every fly around. Granted, he was handsome and popular, but why did the older girls have to put the moves on him? He was just fifteen and she worried about all this attention from them.

I have to trust him.

First she might have to glue her tongue to the roof of her mouth.

In the car, Shane turned to face her. "We were just talking, Mom."

"I know."

"Oh." Surprise filled his blue eyes. Her dad was right. He knew right from wrong and she had to trust her influence would help him make the right choices. But she was so afraid that, just as she had, he would make those choices for all the wrong reasons. How did she tell her teenage son to take it slow? That he had his whole life ahead of him?

She wanted to keep him safe and protect him from life's harsh realities. The only way to do that was to be there for him without being critical or judgmental. Good luck with that one, she told herself.

"Mom."

She realized Shane was talking to her. "What?"

"Why were you late? Rebecca Lynn Howard is always on time. Right, Mom?"

She shot him a glance, but didn't comment as she stopped for traffic. "I had an emergency." She told him about Hank.

"Wow, is he gonna be okay?"

"Yes. He just needs medical treatment."

Shane pushed up straight in his seat. "Do you think Luke will be doing the hiring at the Circle C now?"

"I have no idea," Becky replied, turning on the county road that led home. "Why?"

"He's cool. He might hire me."

She ignored the panic rising in her chest. "Between school, homework and sports, you do not have time for a job."

"But I will this summer and I could buy some cool kind of truck when my birthday rolls around."

"Your birthday isn't until the end of December and we'll discuss the truck then. Right now let's concentrate on getting you out of tenth grade."

And away from older girls.

"Ah, Mo-om." He slumped in his seat.

Sometimes she believed he thought more about trucks than he did about girls. It was a comforting thought.

IT WAS LATE WHEN LUKE and his parents finally made it home. After Hank had been stabilized in the E.R., the doctor had come out and told them he was going to be fine, but they were going to keep him overnight for observation. And they wanted to keep him on oxygen for twenty-four hours.

Hank was resting comfortably in a room with Marla and Chelsea by his side. The way it should be. Luke didn't know why Hank couldn't see he should be with his wife and daughter.

Hap and Clover were waiting at the kitchen table. "How's Hank?" Hap got to his feet.

"He's going to be fine," Luke answered.

"Good." Hap slapped Luke on the back. "We make a good team, boy."

"What do you mean?" Henry asked.

"Well, I noticed Hank's horse was riderless and I knew something was wrong, then Luke landed the chopper and dove into the creek. I followed along the creek bed until I found them."

"Good thing you roped us, Hap. I was running out of strength and we both probably would have drowned."

Henry touched his shoulder. "Are you okay, son?"

"Yeah, Pa." Not once during the evening had Henry asked the same about Hank. He seemed more annoyed with him than concerned. There was a lot going on Luke didn't understand. Why was there always such tension between Henry and Hank?

Sixteen years had changed nothing.

"Honey, it's been a long day." Lucy spoke

to Henry. "And it's time for you to be in bed."

Henry frowned. "Don't treat me like an invalid again, Lu."

"Okay." Lucy lifted an eyebrow. "You can put me to bed, then, because I'm exhausted."

His father grinned as his mom slipped her arm through his. "'Night all," Lucy called as they headed down the hall.

Luke sank into a chair in the den.

"Do you want a cup of coffee?" Clover asked.

"Nah. I'm wired enough."

Hap took a seat. "Tell Hank not to worry. The calves are in the feed lots and their mamas are in one of the north pastures. Everything's done."

"Thanks, Hap. I'm sure he'll be asking." Luke ran his hands over his face. "I'm exhausted, too. Think I'll go up and pass out for the night."

"How about a bite to eat?" Clover asked.

"No, thanks. We ate at the hospital." He rose to his feet. "See y'all in the morning."

Luke fell across his bed, totally spent. He could see the window and the darkness outside—it seemed like a void, but he knew it held something deep and complex. It triggered flashes of the crash and that falling, helpless feeling. He felt the tautness in his gut and fought the nightmare waiting to claim him.

Flipping over, he saw Becky's face as the rain splattered on her face and caused her hair to frizz around her forehead. One fear was replaced with another. He was never going to get over Rebecca Lynn Parker.

BECKY SAT on the stoop staring at the black sky and its sparks of light—God's cathedral lit by a million stars too breathtaking to describe. She wished she could pluck one from the orbit and keep it in her pocket to guide her when she didn't have a clue where she was going.

Like now.

Her first instinct was to protect her son, as she had for fifteen years. Now she was going to be the one to hurt him. She didn't know how to stop that, but she knew without a doubt she had to reveal her secret.

To Shane.

And to Luke.

She bit down on her lip and tasted the blood on her tongue. *God, how could I have made so many wrong decisions?* Looking back, she thought she'd needed a star in her pocket back then. She'd made decisions based solely on her emotions and not sound reasoning.

How could she undo that?

With the truth.

It was so simple, yet so incredibly hard. The truth would change her life forever. It would change her relationship with her son. And Luke would hate her for the rest of his life.

The screen door opened and her father stepped out. "You've been out here a long time. It's cold."

Becky hadn't even noticed the temperature. "I was just thinking."

Hub eased down beside her. "What about?"

"The truth."

"Mmm. That's a toughie."

"I've guarded my secret for so many years and I believe I've kept it for a very good reason. I thought Luke didn't love me."

"I know."

"But if I had to do it over again, I would still love Luke. I would still have Shane."

"That's the trouble with truth. It reveals something basic inside us that's hard to understand."

That was probably the most profound thing her father had ever said. Again she wondered why she hadn't trusted him when she was seventeen. He'd trusted her.

"Danny said it's time and he's right. I can't keep this secret any longer. The coward in me wants to tuck it away and keep it hidden forever. I realize my instinct is to protect myself and I've been doing that all along— protecting myself from any more pain. Now I have to think about Shane and do what's right. But telling him will be the hardest thing I've ever had to do." She wiped away a tear.

Hub patted her knee. "Like I told you, Rebecca, Shane knows we love him and that will get him through a lot of rough patches. Luke Chisum, that's another story."

The second-hardest thing she would ever have to do.

"When he was a teenager, he was like a lit firecracker waiting to explode," her father went on. "But since he's come home, I've sensed a change in him. He's different, more mature. So you might be surprised by his reaction."

"Maybe." She seriously doubted it, though. Luke had changed in a lot of ways, but hearing she'd kept his son from him wasn't going to set well.

Hub got to his feet. "I'm turning in. Don't sit out here too long."

"I won't. Good night."

Hub paused. "Rebecca…"

"I know, Daddy. You're always here for me."

"Yep. Don't ever forget that."

As the screen door banged shut, Becky made a solemn vow that she would never forget what her father had done for her. One person would be by her side through all the turmoil that was to come.

Her friend Annie would be there, too. So would Molly and Tessa, her new friends. And Rachel. They hadn't been close in high school, but they'd formed a new connection—a stronger, adult one.

She reached one hand toward the sky and plucked an imaginary star from its setting. Her hand curled into a fist and she stuffed it into the pocket of her jeans. A make-believe keepsake she would take with her to guide her words as she explained the past to her son.

And to Luke.

CHAPTER EIGHT

MARLA BROUGHT HANK HOME on Sunday afternoon. Luke thought a calm, thankful man would be returning to the house. He'd been wrong. Hank barked orders at everyone, including Marla and Chelsea, who had come along for the ride.

Hank sank into a chair in the den with a frown.

"I tried to talk him into staying in San Antonio for a few days but he wouldn't listen to me." Marla hugged Lucy, and asked, "How are you, Henry?"

"Fine. Doin' better every day."

"I'm glad to hear that."

Chelsea kissed her grandfather's cheek and hugged her grandmother.

"Why don't you stay for a while?" Lucy's eyes filled with love as she stared at her granddaughter.

"Oh, Grandma. I wish I could, but I have

classes tomorrow. I promise I'll come for a long weekend soon. Hey, unc." Chelsea winked at Luke.

He held out his arms and she ran into them. He swung her around and her laughter filled the room.

"Put her down, Luke," Hank scolded. "She's not a kid."

Chelsea rolled her eyes as Luke set her on her feet. She was a blond beauty like her mother, except she'd inherited the brown eyes of her father. Luke hoped that was all she'd inherited from Hank.

"We'd better go," Marla said, glancing at her husband. "You sure you won't change your mind and spend the week in San Antonio with me?"

"You never seem to understand I work here and here is where I need to be."

"But you need some time to recuperate."

"There's nothing wrong with me. I swallowed some creek water. So what? And if Luke hadn't pounded on my chest so damn hard, I wouldn't have a problem breathing."

"Excuse me? I was trying to save your life."

"I think you were trying to kill me."

Luke threw up his hands and walked out

of the room before he said something he'd regret. At the moment, he did feel like killing the ungrateful lout. Outside, he took several deep breaths to calm himself.

Chelsea followed him. "Don't pay any attention to Dad. He's been barking at Mom and me all weekend." She leaned close and whispered, "I'm tired of playing referee."

Luke smiled at her. "You know, I think Marla must have had an affair because you can't be Hank's daughter."

"Let's don't tell anyone that," she added in that same whisper, and then burst out laughing. Luke laughed with her.

Chelsea reminded him of a cola that had been shaken vigorously, all bubbles and fizz. And fun.

Marla opened the door. "Let's go, Chel, before I hurt your father."

"Okeydokey." Chelsea made a face.

"I'm sorry, Luke," Marla said.

"Don't worry about it. I'm used to it."

"Yes, and we shouldn't be."

After they left, Luke felt a need to get away. He jumped into his truck and drove to Cross Fox Ranch. Seeing Brady at the track, he headed there.

"Luke," Brady called.

Living close, he and Brady had grown up together and they knew the bad and the good about the other. Luke was on leave when Brady's gig in Vegas had ended in tragedy. As soon as Luke got the call, he was on a plane to Vegas and he and Brady had flown home, leaving the bad memories behind.

Brady was finally getting his life straight and Luke was happy for him. He and Molly were made for each other.

Luke got out and walked over to him. They leaned on the fence watching Dobbs, the horse trainer, putting Amber Mac through his paces. Cross Fox Ranch was a third-generation Thoroughbred training facility. One day Brady would take over the reins, but first he had to prove to his father he was home to stay and he had what it took to train a winning horse. Amber Mac was Brady's chance.

"He looks good," Luke commented, watching the long strides of the chestnut Thoroughbred.

"You're damn straight he is," Brady boasted with pride. "He's going to be a winner for me, Luke." His gaze swung to him. "What are you doing over here on a Sunday afternoon?"

"I just needed some air."

"Damn, Luke, are you and your brother ever going to get along?"

"Probably not." He told his friend about the near-drowning experience.

"That's rough, man," Brady said. "Let's go into town and get a beer."

"What about Molly?"

"She and my mom are in San Antonio shopping. Dad and Sammy are fishing so it's the perfect time. I could use a break, too. Just let me tell Dobbs."

"I'll meet you at the Scoot 'n' Boot," Luke shouted on the way to his truck. This was what he needed—to be with his friend and to forget about his lousy screwed-up life.

As he pulled up to the bar, Brady braked to a stop beside him. When they were younger, they'd race into town to see who could get there first. What a difference the years had made. Maturity had finally arrived for the Wild Bunch.

They walked into the rustic tavern, their boots sounding like sandpaper on the concrete floor. Duct tape covered worn holes in the red vinyl booths and the bar stools. The long bar was tarnished, years of scratches marring its surface. Faded wood tables fittingly sported mismatched chairs.

Sitting at one of the tables were Blake, Cole and Jake.

"Hey, y'all can't drink without us," Brady said, grabbing a chair.

Luke did the same.

"What are you guys doing in town on a Sunday afternoon?" Brady asked.

"Jake helped me center a beam on the ceiling of the bar," Cole replied. "Blake and Annie had dinner with Mom, then Blake came to give us a hand and let me tell you, I needed every hand I could get. With my bad ankle, shinnying up a ladder isn't as easy as it used to be.

"We decided it was time for a beer," Cole added. "What brings y'all into town?"

"Same thing—beer," Luke replied, signaling the waitress.

"Whatda you want, Luke?" Thelma Sue, the waitress, shouted from the bar.

Luke held up two fingers. "Beer."

"No place like home, is there, boys?" Brady said, smiling. "Whatever happened to the Elly May–type barmaids?"

"This is River Bluff," Cole reminded him.

"Yeah, and we have someone old enough to be our mothers in orthopedic shoes." Jake rested his forearms on the table with a smile.

Blake took a swallow from his bottle. "It's a refreshing change from the pace of big-city life."

Thelma Sue set two frosty cold bottles on the table. "Is this together or separate?" she asked, smacking on gum.

"Together," Blake answered before anyone else could.

Thelma Sue winked. "You got it."

"You came all the way into town for a beer?" Jake asked.

"Sure. Luke needed to unwind." Brady reached for his bottle.

"Why?" Jake asked and then held up a hand. "Wait—brother or Becky?"

"Brother," Luke muttered and told them what had happened.

"God, that's awful." Cole set down his beer. "Is he okay? Are you okay?"

"I'm not sure," Luke admitted, running his thumb over the cool wetness of the label. "As I was trying to save him, it brought back so many memories of rescues in Iraq, the horror and the sense-less pain."

There was complete silence around the table. Luke realized for the first time how heavily those memories weighed on his mind. From the look on his friends' faces, he knew they worried about him.

Blake patted his shoulder. "Are you having nightmares?"

"Sometimes." He had no problem admitting that.

"I can recommend a good counselor."

"I saw one at Reed and he told me it was going to take time."

"Maybe…"

"I'm fine, Blake," he cut in. "It's Hank's bullshit that ties me up in knots and brings it back. I can handle it though."

"Just don't go driving any cars off cliffs," Jake joked.

"I've outgrown that." Luke toyed with his bottle. "You know, you guys are the cause of my insanity. You were the ones who told me I couldn't make that Mustang fly and you were the ones who dared me to date Becky. Maybe I need to find new friends."

"Yeah." Brady laughed. "Who would have you?"

"Mmm. You have a point." Luke took a swallow. "I'm an expert at screwing up my own life. I'm thirty-four and wondering what the hell I'm going to do with the rest of my life."

There was silence for a moment.

"Play Texas Hold 'Em," Jake hazarded a guess, grinning.

Luke raised his bottle. "That sounds about right."

They clinked their beers. "To poker," they chorused in unison.

Then Jake added, "To second chances."

"To a new baby," Blake said.

"To home and family." Cole raised his bottle high.

"To a new life and may it be a winner, both on the track and off." Brady wasn't going to be outdone.

They all looked at Luke.

"To the road ahead," was all he could say. His friends' futures were clear, but his own was as muddy as the Medina River after a rainstorm.

When Luke reached home, the house was dark and quiet. He tiptoed upstairs and fell into bed, refusing to think any more about his life. If he did, his head was going to split open. But try as he might, he couldn't help but wonder what the road ahead held for him.

MONDAY WAS TENSE. Hank insisted on saddling up. Lucy talked and pleaded to no avail. Henry was no help. He said, "Let the boy do what he wants. He's a grown man."

So Luke spent the day keeping an eye on Hank and that irritated the hell out of Luke. His brother should have had enough sense to take care of himself. But no matter how angry Luke was, Hank was never out of his or Hap's sight.

The evening meal was even tenser. Not much was said. Clover usually ate with them, but tonight she went to her room off the kitchen. Wise woman. No one wanted to be around Hank.

Luke couldn't understand why Hank was so angry. Most people were usually grateful after someone had saved their life. But not Hank. He seemed to resent it. Or it could be he just resented that it had been Luke who'd saved him.

Henry pushed back his plate. "I want to talk to you boys." He reached for his cane and made his way into the den.

Luke had a bad feeling in his gut about out-of-the-blue talk, but he made his way into the den.

Henry and Hank sat in their chairs. Luke took the leather sofa.

"Henry, don't you think this can wait?"

Lucy seemed nervous and that bad feeling intensified.

"No, Lucy, I should have done this years ago," Henry replied.

"What are you talking about?" Hank wanted to know.

"I've been doing a lot of thinking since you almost drowned. We never know when our time is coming. I could die tonight. So could your mother. I want my affairs in order when that happens. I spoke with Jonathan Turner today."

"Your lawyer?" Hank asked.

"Yes. He's drawing up a deed of trust for the Circle C. As of today I no longer own the ranch—half belongs to Hank and the other half goes to Luke."

Hank jumped to his feet. "What!"

"It's a done deal, boy."

"You promised. You said you wouldn't do this." The blood vessels on Hank's neck stood out in anger.

"Things change."

"You've changed. That's all. Luke doesn't deserve half of this ranch and you know it."

"He does," Henry shouted. "He's my son."

"Like hell he is."

"Hank, please." Lucy tried to calm him.

Hank turned to her. "Dad said when you brought Luke home the adoption didn't change anything. This ranch would always be mine." His dark eyes pierced Henry. "Guess you lied."

"It's a done deal, Hank. Give it up." Henry's jaw clenched.

"Yeah, that's just about it." Hank's chest expanded rapidly. "I gave up everything and not a day goes by I don't regret that. I listened to you, but this is it. Luke can have the ranch. I'm outta here."

"No." Luke was on his feet, feeling as if he were in the twilight zone or some bizarre place other than the family den. "You can have the ranch, Hank. I don't want it."

"See what your pampering has done, Pa. He doesn't even care about this place and I've put my blood, sweat and tears into it."

"I care about it," Luke snapped. "But I'm not taking anything away from you that makes you this angry. I can survive without this ranch. You can't."

"Then you're not a Chisum."

The truth of those words slammed into Luke's heart like a sledgehammer and he had trouble breathing. No one had ever said those words out loud to him before.

"Please, stop this," Lucy begged.

"I'm gone," Hank said, moving toward the back door.

"Hank." Lucy ran after him.

Luke faced his father. "Why did you do that? Why did you have to do that?"

"It had to be done," was his stubborn response.

"Well, undo it. I don't want half of this ranch. It belongs to Hank. He's a Chisum."

"You're a Chisum, boy, and don't you ever forget it."

No matter how many times Henry said that, it wasn't going to make it true. Luke didn't know how to get through to his father, but he had to keep trying. "Call your lawyer and stop this. It'll tear apart this family, can't you see that?"

Those tired brown eyes stared right at him. "It's time for you to stand up and take responsibility. It's time for you to be a man. It's time to prove you're a Chisum."

"God, is your head made of stone?" Luke gritted his teeth in frustration.

"Someday, boy, you'll understand."

"I don't think I'll ever understand this kind of hurtful meanness." Saying that, he headed for the door.

He met his mother. "Where's Hank?"

"He's gone. I couldn't stop him."

"Damn." He glanced back at his dad. "Why didn't you try to stop him from doing this?"

"Don't you think I've tried? I've talked until I'm blue in the face."

He sagged, feeling the weight of everything closing in on him. "I don't understand any of this."

"I'm sorry, Luke."

"I have to get out of here.

"Luke…"

He yanked open the door and snapped it shut behind him. Becky stood on the step, her hand raised toward the knob, her eyes startled.

"Becky, what are you doing here?"

"Your mother called and said she was worried about Henry."

"Pa's fine. He's just stubborn as an ox." He swung toward the backyard, not really wanting to talk—not even to Becky.

Becky wasn't sure what was going on so she followed Luke for answers. He sat on the swing under the old oak tree, his face buried in his hands. Her stomach clenched.

"Luke."

"Go away. I don't want to talk."

Usually she would have heeded the warning in his voice. Talking to Luke wasn't something she did easily. She was afraid she'd reveal too much. But tonight she sat beside him. The swing squeaked and it brought back memories of other times she'd sat here with Luke.

Moonlight spilled across the yard and she glanced up to the massive canopy and millions of tiny lights that always calmed her and gave her strength. She placed her fist over the pocket of her jeans.

"What happened?" she asked quietly.

To her surprise he removed his hands from his face and stared off into the darkness. At first she didn't think he was going to speak, but slowly he began to tell her about Henry deeding the ranch to Hank and Luke, and Hank's reaction to it.

"I don't want it," he said. "It belongs to Hank."

"Why do you say that?"

"Hank's a Chisum and this is Chisum land—has been for over a hundred years."

"But you're a Chisum."

"Only by adoption—not by blood."

"Adoption is legally binding, Luke. It makes you a Chisum."

He stood and jammed his hands through his hair. "Not to Hank."

"Why are you so concerned about Hank's feelings?"

"I don't know. I just am and I don't want to be the cause of a rift in this family. I have the urge to leave again, to get away from it all."

"You're leaving?" She was unable to keep the panic out of her voice. It hit her then. She didn't want him to leave. For years she'd worried about him, especially when he'd been in Iraq. When she'd heard about the crash, she couldn't sleep for three days wondering what he was going through. And if he was going to be okay. And if he was coming home. For good?

All that worry got derailed by thoughts of her son. Luke's son. How long could she keep that secret from him? How long could she continue to lie? She knew she had to tell him, but if he was leaving…

She could feel his eyes on her. "You sound as if you don't want me to leave," he remarked.

Her fist tightened on the pocket of her jeans. "I don't," she said, feeling a tremor run through her at that admission.

"Then give me a reason to stay."

CHAPTER NINE

SHE HAD THE PERFECT OPENING. All she had to do was say the words, but something held her back.

Fear.

Uncertainty.

And the unknown. She didn't know how Luke was going to react to the information after Hank's open anger at him. He was dealing with enough and she wanted him calm and in control when she told him.

She'd gone over this so many times, the wording, the timing, the setting. In truth, though, her hesitation had a lot to do with Luke's reaction to her—she didn't want him to hate her.

"Becky."

His voice wrapped around her, as enticing as the lure of the moonlight. The feeling she'd experienced the other day in his bedroom surfaced. She wanted to kiss him—to feel week-in-the-knees magic that had made her feel sexy and alive and the most important person in the world. To him.

Suddenly it was more important to make that connection they'd had years ago. She rose and took several steps until she was a breath away from him. She stood on tiptoes and ran her hands up his broad chest to tangle in the hair at the nape of his neck. Warm, forgotten pleasure ran through her body at the touch of his masculine skin. She breathed in the musky scent of him.

Crickets chirped and the cool breeze rumbled through the trees, but she didn't notice. All she heard was the pounding of her blood in her ears.

His head bent and he kissed her cheek, the corner of her mouth and slowly took her lips, savoring that first erotic, stimulating touch after being apart for so many years. The magic was still there. Her knees buckled as he deepened the kiss, his mouth covering hers completely. Her arms tightened around his neck and his locked around her like steel bands.

She moaned as the kiss went on. It reached deep inside her to that special place she kept only for him—her heart. The taste of his lips, his skin was the same; familiar and a part of her. She pressed closer, needing to feel every inch of him.

"Oh, sweet Bec," he groaned, his hands caressing her back and lower. "I…"

"Luke, where are you?" His mother's voice was like a douse of cold water and it brought back so many memories of Lucy finding them necking.

Luke said a curse word and rested his forehead on hers. "Bec…"

"It's okay." Unable to resist, she cupped his face with one hand, loving the rough texture of his skin and his stubble against her palm. "We'll talk later."

They walked toward the door and Becky wanted to grab his hand and hold on to the feeling just a moment longer.

What am I doing?

The wind chilled her skin, taking away all that warmth. How had she gotten sidetracked into satisfying some emotional need inside her? She had to focus on Shane. But right now every nerve ending was centered on Luke.

"What is it, Mom?" Luke asked as they reached her, standing at the entrance to the backyard with her arms wrapped around her waist.

"I was looking for Becky. Her car is here and I knew she had to be with you. Your father's blood pressure is high and I'm worried."

"I'll check him," Becky said, walking around Luke to the door.

They entered the house. "Where's Henry?"

"He's in the bedroom," Lucy replied. "I finally got him to lie down. This is all just nonsense, but you can't tell a Chisum anything."

Luke sank into a chair in the breakfast room as Becky and his mother headed for the hall. He touched his lips. Becky had kissed him. He'd been waiting six months for that. Hell, he'd been waiting sixteen years for that. It was better than he'd ever remembered in his countless sleepless nights and unforgettable dreams. There was no resentment in her kiss or her touch. He could still feel her rounded curves against him. She wanted him to stay in River Bluff. He took a minute to mull over that.

What had happened in a matter of a few days to make her want him to stay? He'd thought she'd wanted him at the farthest end of the earth. Her kiss didn't say that.

He really wasn't leaving. He'd just had the feeling the way he had so many times in his youth when he and Hank had argued. Back then he'd get lost on the Circle C or do something dangerous—until he'd made the momentous decision to leave for good. Tonight he'd asked Becky for a reason for him to stay and she'd given him a good one.

Could they forget the past and build a future as adults? That was what he wanted, just like when he was eighteen. But he'd been too young then to face those bumps in the road that came with life. They'd been just kids in love with their heads full of dreams.

Dreams that came with a price.

A price tag of truth and forgiveness.

As teenagers, they couldn't accomplish that, but now they could. They had a second chance.

Clover, in her housecoat, stomped from her room, her gray hair standing on end as if she'd fallen asleep watching TV.

"Hey, Clo."

She opened the refrigerator and reached for a milk carton. "Fireworks display over?"

"For now," he told her.

"There's too much tension in this house." She poured milk into a glass.

"Yeah. At times I wish I hadn't come home."

"With Becky here, how likely is that?" She put the milk back in the fridge and left without another word.

Was he so transparent? Did everyone know how he felt about Becky?

His mother walked in and sat down at the table.

"How's Pa?"

"Fine. These kinds of upsets are not good for him though. We got him to the hospital in time when he had the stroke. That's why he's doing so well. I'm just afraid we won't be so lucky the next time."

"He's doing it to himself, Mom. There was no need to deed the land over now."

"Son, when are you going to realize this is your heritage?"

"Hank doesn't see it that way."

"Then Hank has some adjusting to do."

Luke shifted uncomfortably, but he had to ask some hard questions because none of this was making any sense to him. "Why is there such animosity between Pa and Hank?"

"It's hard to explain."

"Try me."

"Hank has been upset since the day we brought you home. He didn't want a little brother and that made Henry angry."

"So Pa forced Hank to accept me?"

"Sort of." Lucy folded her hands on the table. "It's just been one thing after another. Henry blamed Hank that time you fell off the cattle trailer and had a concussion and twenty stitches in your head."

Luke frowned. "I was six and climbing on everything. How could Pa blame him for that?"

"Hank was supposed to be watching you."

"Mom, that's ridiculous. I was a kid."

"Exactly. Hank was the adult and we trusted him to take care of you." Lucy waved a hand. "But it's so much more than that. Henry blamed Hank when you crashed the Mustang, too."

"That was more about Becky and how I hurt her. I didn't know how to deal with my feelings."

Lucy nodded. "Your father blamed Hank for your joining the army."

"What?"

"Every day I prayed you'd come back alive because if anything happened to you it would kill all of us."

Luke got up and squatted in front of Lucy, taking her hands in his. "I'm sorry, Mom. I had to go. I couldn't stay here and watch Becky and Danny together."

She touched his face. "I know, son."

"Hank's on my case all the time about this ranch. Let him have it. By right it's his. And I don't want him to hate me forever."

"I wish it was that simple, but it's not. You're our son, too, and Hank has to accept that."

Luke shook his head. "It hasn't happened in thirty-four years and it's not going to happen now."

"Yes, it will." Lucy bobbed her head in the affirmative. "But I'm worried about Hank. I want you to go and find your brother."

"I'm the last person Hank wants to see."

"Still, I want you to go. I called Marla and he's not there, but he will be. He always goes to Marla. Tell him we love him."

"Mom." Luke stood in an angry movement.

"Are you going, or not?" Those mother's eyes held him like the beam of a spotlight he couldn't escape.

"Oh, okay. I'll go first thing in the morning."

"No. I want you to go tonight."

"Mom, God, let's give him a break." Luke had other reasons for not going tonight, too. He wanted to talk to Becky.

"Luke." That beam was scorching his resolve and his patience.

He dragged in a breath. "Okay."

"Tell him we love him and want him to come home."

He lifted an eyebrow. "Are you sure about the *we* part?"

"Luke Chisum." The wattage of the beam was now burning at full power.

"Yes, ma'am." He felt six years old again, but if she wanted him to bring Hank home then he'd try. And trying was going to get him the biggest tongue-lashing of his life. But what was a guy to do when his mother was pleading with him?

He'd rather sneak off and be with Becky.

That wasn't going to happen, though. They had a lot of talking to do first and they didn't have to sneak around anymore.

Becky came into the breakfast room and Luke turned to her. Auburn hair framed her face and her blue eyes were as bright as he'd ever seen them. He could still taste her on his lips—a very good trick of his imagination.

"How's Pa?" he asked.

"His blood pressure is down and he's asleep. Getting upset is not in his best interest, health-wise."

"I hope you told him that."

"Yes, but it didn't seem to make a difference. He's adamant about things he says have to be done."

"He's a stubborn man, but thank you, Becky." Lucy stood and kissed Becky's cheek. "I don't know what I'd do without you." She glanced at Luke and she didn't have to say a word. Luke knew what she was thinking.

Why are you still here?

"I'm going."

"Good." She touched his cheek and left the room.

"Where are you going?" Becky walked to within two feet of him and he could smell the lemony soap she used to wash her hands. It was the most erotic scent he'd ever smelled. It wrapped him in memories of the kiss—a willing kiss from Becky.

"To find Hank," he replied, realizing she was waiting for an answer.

"Really?" Her lips twitched slightly into a grin. "So you're staying?"

"You gave me a good reason to stay, didn't you?" He found he was holding his breath as he waited for her answer.

"I would hate for you to run from River Bluff once again, to run from your problems. I would rather you stayed and faced them."

That wasn't exactly what he wanted to hear and it must have shown on his face. She quickly added, "If you had stayed sixteen years ago, things might be different today. But we can't go back and change anything. We have to go forward. I'm now able to do that."

"Me, too."

She smiled one of her Becky smiles, and the blood rushed through his veins in a re-membered fever.

He couldn't help but grin. He hadn't seen her smile like that in years. "After I chase Hank down and we sort out this family situa-tion, how about a quiet dinner and a movie? A date—" his grin broadened "—without a dare."

"Sounds nice," she replied, glancing at her watch. "I've got to go. I've left Shane doing his homework and he tends to get sidetracked if I'm not there."

She had a kid—a whole other life without him. He wasn't going to dwell on that, though. He was going to make the most of this opportunity.

"I'll call you tomorrow."

"Okay," she said, but didn't move.

Neither of them did.

With one hand, he encircled her neck and pulled her toward him, his lips taking hers in a gentle caress. That lasted for about a second. He groaned and covered her mouth, tasting her sweetness and everything that was Becky. It was powerful, passionate and he had a hard time stopping, but he had to. This time he wanted to do everything right.

"Oh, Bec," he whispered.

"I know," she breathed against his lips. "It's different, but still the same."

"Mmm." He kissed the side of her neck.

"I have to go," she murmured raggedly.

"Then do it quickly."

With one last lingering kiss, she ran for the door.

Luke drew a deep breath and spun around, feeling as giddy as a kid. Things were finally going his way.

Well, almost.

Now he had to find his neurotic brother.

BECKY RESTED her forehead on the steering wheel, feeling its coolness.

What am I doing?

She couldn't answer that question. It just felt right to kiss him. She ignored all the warning voices in her head and went with her heart. That was so wrong.

She started the engine, then headed for home. She wanted them to be friends so she could tell him about Shane, but she was leading him on with half-truths when she should have told him the honest-to-God truth. In high school, she'd been so devastated when Luke hadn't told her the truth. Now she was doing the same thing to him. And it wasn't for revenge.

She was a coward—postponing the inevitable because she didn't have the courage to admit her mistakes. The undeniable truth stared her in the face. She was weak, clinging to memories in hopes they would soften the blow.

I'm a coward.

Driving up to her house, she thought how much easier it would be if she just kept her secret. But that wasn't an option anymore. This time she would not take the coward's way out. She would find the strength to reveal the truth and pray for mercy.

As she entered the house, she heard the TV blaring. Hub was asleep in his recliner, the remote in his hand. She turned down the sound and didn't wake her father. He fussed at having his sleep disturbed, so she left him alone.

She walked to her son's room. He lay on the floor in pajama bottoms, his feet propped on the bed. An iPod earbud was stuck in his ear and he moved his body to the beat of the music. His school books were strewn around him and he flipped through a magazine.

Oh God, not another girlie magazine.

She reached down and removed the earbud.

He turned to her with a startled gaze, but made no effort to hide the magazine, so she knew it wasn't one of those she disliked him looking through. Or drooling over.

"Hey, Mom," he said cheerfully.

"Are you finished with your homework?"

"Yep." He sat up, all arms and legs. "And Mrs. Harvey is going to be blown away by the paper I've written. It's an A for sure."

"May I read it please?"

"Sure." He searched around on the floor and picked up a sheet of paper. "The project was to express our views on something we're passionate about."

"Really?"

"Yeah, Mom. I wrote about trucks." He handed her the paper.

She sat on the bed, trying not to smile. Her eyes focused on the typed assignment. There was a stain on one corner—probably peanut butter. Her son loved peanut butter.

My dream truck was the title. And on he wrote about the truck of his dreams. Greta Harvey wasn't going to understand half of it because Becky didn't. It was about engines, horsepower, torque and the must-have four-wheel drive. The paper was good. Shane had expressed his feelings and that was what Greta had wanted.

"It's good," she told him.

"And look, Mom." He reached for a photo and sprang to his feet. "I have a picture, too." He sat beside her and showed her. "It's a red F-350 Ford Lariat dually, crew cab, diesel, fully loaded with tons of sharp-looking chrome trim, leather interior, state-of-the-art stereo system, satellite radio, four-wheel drive, all-terrain tires and a sticker price of forty-four thousand dollars. Is that a dream or what?"

"Definitely a dream." She experienced a moment of sadness. She would never be able to afford anything like this for Shane. Not that he needed a truck that expensive, nor was he likely to get one. Still, dreams were hard to let go, especially for a young boy. And she wanted her son to have everything.

She bit her lip as she realized she was going to crush his whole world. How was she supposed to do that?

"I'm very proud of you."

"Ah, Mom." He took the photo and paper and stuffed it in a folder. She wanted to tell him to reprint the paper because of the stain, but for some reason she didn't. Greta wouldn't take off for it.

He slipped from the bed and gathered his books, poking them into his backpack.

She took a deep breath. "Shane, everything I do, I do in your best interest. You do know that, don't you?"

He glanced up, confusion in his eyes. "Yeah. I guess."

"But I make mistakes."

He thought about that for a minute. "Like

the time you decided we had too many carbs in our diet—right before Thanksgiving." He rolled his eyes. "We had turkey and broccoli and something I don't even want to think about anymore." He shuddered in disgust.

"It was pretty awful."

"And Grandpa and I didn't get pumpkin pie."

"I made it for you later."

"But it wasn't the same."

No, it wasn't, but that bizarre Thanksgiving didn't even touch what she had to tell him. She took another breath.

He stood and brushed hair out of his eyes. Tall and muscled, he was starting to sprout some fuzzy hairs on his chest. He was becoming a man. How did that happen so fast? Yesterday, he was a little boy pushing toy trucks on the floor, making engine noises.

"Is that what you mean by mistakes?"

She locked her fingers together. "I just want you to know I'm not perfect."

"Jeez, Mom." He plopped down beside her. "Are you sick or something?"

"No. I'm fine." She looked into his blue eyes. "I just want to make all the right decisions for you."

"Okay." His eyes twinkled. "No more weird Thanksgivings and if you really want to make my day, you can buy me that red truck."

She kissed his forehead. "Dream on, hotshot."

"Ah, Mom."

She walked to the door and glanced back as he crawled into bed. "'Night, son."

"'Night," he mumbled.

She flipped off the light and hurried to her room. She couldn't do it. The time wasn't right. Picking up the phone, she called Annie. They talked for thirty minutes and Becky felt better.

After taking a shower, she slipped into bed. The tears came then. She cried for all the mistakes she'd made. She cried for the two people her mistakes hurt the most. In the end, she cried for herself. She cried until there were no more tears.

As she drifted into sleep, she felt Luke's lips on her skin.

CHAPTER TEN

HANK'S TRUCK WASN'T at Marla's so Luke drove around the block trying to figure out where his brother would go. A bar. He checked several he'd heard Hank mention, but the King Ranch truck was nowhere to be found.

About two in the morning he parked outside Marla's and waited. He must have dozed off because when he woke up the sun was lazily peeping through the clouds. A hazy yellow light bathed the neighborhood.

He yawned and stretched, feeling the stiffness in his neck and shoulders. Damn! Sleeping in a truck wasn't the most comfortable thing, especially sitting up with his neck at an odd angle.

Damn Hank.

And after that—Hank still wasn't at Marla's. Where in the hell was he?

Through his frustration, Luke realized he

needed to go to the bathroom and he really needed a cup of coffee. He started the truck and drove to a convenience store. After using the restroom, he bought a coffee and a couple of soft tacos. San Antonio had the best Mexican food. A mariachi band played on a radio in the background. The lively beat revived his drooping demeanor. He did a fast cha-cha out the door.

Feeling better, he drove back to Marla's and ate his tacos, waiting. He wasn't sure how much longer he was going to do this. Not one more minute, was his next thought. What the hell was he going to say to Hank, anyway?

Suddenly the garage door went up and Chelsea backed out her Camry. She was talking on her cell phone and didn't even see him parked there. The girl was not observant. The garage door glided down.

He started his truck and whipped into the driveway. Marla had to be up and she was the best person to ask where Hank might hide out. He rang the doorbell.

Marla's voice came from the intercom system. "Who is it?"

"Luke," he replied.

"Oh, Luke. I'm not dressed and I don't have on my makeup."

"It doesn't matter. I need to talk to you about Hank."

"Very few people have seen me without makeup."

"Stop being vain and let me in."

"Stop being a Chisum," she retorted, but he heard the latch being undone. "Brace yourself."

She opened the door and he stared, trying very hard not to react. Marla was dressed in a cream silky negligee, and her hair hung limply to her shoulders. Her eyebrows were blond, as were her eyelashes. The only color on her face was the blue of her eyes.

He lifted an eyebrow. "So what's the problem? You're beautiful, as always." As a good poker player, Luke was able to lie with a straight face.

"Liar," she said, holding the door wider. "I look like an old hag before I put on the war paint, as Hank calls it."

Luke walked into the Tuscany-decorated living room. The trim was dark with sunwashed walls and marble flooring. Everything had an antique look and feel. Somehow he couldn't picture Hank here, with his muddy boots and who-cares attitude. The house was picture-perfect, magazine-style.

And that was something no one would ever call Hank.

They said opposites attract. He supposed that was true. Marla was definitely picture-perfect, except without her makeup. That might take some getting used to. Of course, he wasn't casting stones, because he looked like something the cat dragged in with his rumpled clothes and growth of beard.

He rubbed a hand over the roughness of his chin. "Speaking of Hank, have you heard from him?"

She sank gracefully onto the sofa and crossed her legs. "Not a word."

He sat in a chair that looked and felt like cashmere. Unable to stop himself, he glanced down to make sure his boots were clean. They were.

"Do you know where he might go? Bars? Friends?"

"He does his drinking in River Bluff. When he comes here, it's to see Chelsea and me. He arrives late Saturday afternoon with flowers or some gift he knows I like. We go out to eat and somehow he manages to spend the night and he leaves late on Sunday. I keep telling myself that one Saturday he'll arrive with a suitcase and say he's moving in." She grimaced. "I lie to myself a lot."

Luke rested his elbows on his knees and clasped his hands together. "What keeps him at the ranch?"

She flipped back her hair. "I wish I knew. I used every trick in the book to get him out of there and into a home of our own. Nothing worked, so I left."

"Why didn't you divorce him?" The question was out of line, but it was too late to take it back.

She shrugged. "Foolish. Stupid. Maybe smart. For a woman who made a living with her looks, I knew at my age divorce would be hard on me. It's not as if I would go back to work. I'd been out of the modeling scene too long. And the truth is, I still love Hank so I keep my door open for him, hoping one day he will love me more than some dirt in River Bluff."

"He's an idiot."

"Mmm. But he's my idiot and I'm stuck with him." She straightened the negligee over her knees. "Lucy told me what happened."

"Yeah—the ranch. It's his life and it's killing him that it won't completely be his."

"Hank was never good at sharing."

"If he comes here or calls, tell him I don't want the ranch. It's his, just like Pa promised him. I can deed my part back to him."

She rose in a fluid movement. "That's nice, Luke, but I don't think this is about you and Hank. It's about Hank and Henry. I don't pretend to understand it, but it goes deep and it goes back years."

"My parents' favoring me has a lot to do with it."

"Yes." She gave a fake laugh. "Can you imagine what that's like for Hank, their biological child? Nothing he does is ever good enough for Henry, but all you have to do is just be there."

"I can't change that. I've tried many times."

"It's not up to you, Luke," she told him bluntly. "And for what it's worth, before you turn down your inheritance, you need to think about your life, your future. Legally you are a Chisum and that will hold up in any Texas court."

Someone else had told him the same thing. Becky. He just wanted to get back to her, to make sure he hadn't dreamed last night.

He stood. "I'm beginning to think fighting in Iraq was a piece of cake compared to dealing with the self-inflicted wounds of this family."

"Don't let it get you down. Hank will surface and you'll work things out."

"I don't know, Marla. I've never seen him that angry."

"If he comes here, I'll call you, and if you find him, call me so I can talk to him first."

"Okay. I'd better go and get changed. I'm sure Mom's waiting for a report." He walked toward the door and stopped. "Thanks, Marla."

She smiled. "I'm pretty reasonable considering I don't have on any makeup."

"About that." He grinned. "Next time I'll take your warning more seriously."

"Luke Chisum." She slammed the door in his face.

"Ouch," he yelled, jumping out of harm's way.

"You deserved it," she yelled back.

"Touché."

There was no response, so he headed for his truck.

Where in the hell was Hank?

BACK AT GREAT OAKS, Lucy was full of questions. The fact Hank had managed to disappear without a trace worried her. Henry sat in his chair staring at a blank TV screen. Luke thought it best to let him sulk. He didn't want to get into an argument with his father. Tempers had to cool first.

He hurried upstairs to his room, eager to call Becky. She was on her way to work.

"Good morning," she said and her voice washed over him like warm water. "Did you find Hank?"

"No." He lay back on his bed, just enjoying the sound of her voice. "He's not at Marla's. I'm going into River Bluff to see if anyone has seen him."

"Maybe he just needs some time."

"Trying telling that to my mother."

"She's just worried."

"Yeah." His hand tightened on the phone. "Could we go out tonight? I don't plan to look for Hank much longer."

"Oh, Luke, I'm sorry. On Tuesdays and Wednesdays I work until seven at the clinic and then I have to go home and fix supper for Shane and make sure he does his homework."

"I see." Disappointment filled him. "Wednesday I have the poker game, so I guess we'll have to wait until the weekend."

"I guess."

"Becky…"

"What?"

"Nothing," he replied. "I just like saying your name."

"Oh, Luke, that's so sweet."

"Mmm. Is it okay if I call you tonight?"

"Sure."

He hung up and went to take a shower, smiling.

Forty-five minutes later he was in River Bluff, asking questions. No one had seen Hank. He drove down Main Street and saw Cole and Tessa outside *River Run,* the local newspaper, evidently sharing a goodbye kiss. Tessa had her own consulting firm and she also did some occasional photography work for the paper.

He whipped into a parking space and pushed a button to roll down his window. "Mornin', lovebirds."

"Hey, Luke," Cole said. "You're in town early."

"I'm looking for Hank. Have you seen him?"

Cole shook his head. "No, and to tell you the truth, I give Hank a wide berth. It brings back too many painful memories of him yelling at us for being losers and spending all our time playing poker."

"Poor baby." Tessa stroked his hair and kissed him. "I've got to run, honey. Bye, Luke." She quickly went inside.

Luke watched the expression on Cole's face. "You've got it bad, man."

"Yeah." Cole grinned from ear to ear. "And it's so sweet."

They saw Brady at the same time. He came out of a vacant storefront down the street. "What's Brady up to?" Cole asked.

"I have no idea." Luke opened his door and got out. "Let's ask him."

"Hey, guys," Brady said as they walked up. "Bet you're wondering what I'm doing."

"You could say that," Luke replied, noticing workers inside.

"Molly's opening a kids' used-clothing store and I'm helping out by doing man stuff." He flexed his muscles.

Cole and Luke laughed.

"Didn't know you could do *man stuff*," Luke said, laughter still in his voice.

"Me, neither," Cole added.

"C'mon, guys, I'm not the one who passed out from too much liquor at the House of Red Lights when we were teenagers. Jake and I had to drag y'all out of there and miss a night of debauchery."

"Your memory is so selective," Luke said, trying not to laugh again. "You were puking your guts out in the parking lot."

"Here comes Jake." Brady pointed down the street to Jake pushing a baby stroller with Rachel at his side. "Let's ask him."

"As stimulating as this conversation is, I have to get to work. See y'all Wednesday night." Cole walked to his truck.

"What's up?" Jake asked as he reached them.

"We have a difference of opinion on what happened at the House of Red Lights years ago," Luke told him.

"Good God, y'all still aren't talking about that." Jake held up a hand as Brady started to speak. "Bottom line, boys, we were teenagers, drunk and idiots. Nothing else needs to be said."

"Brady was bragging about his man stuff," Luke remarked.

"Brady's always bragging," Jake said.

"Wait a minute," Brady protested.

"What's the House of Red Lights?" Rachel asked, and quickly shook her head. "No. I can figure that one out for myself."

They laughed and Molly stepped outside. "What's so funny?"

"Nothing," Brady said and winked. "I'll tell you later."

"Whatever." Molly shrugged, glancing at Rachel. "I'm glad you're here. You can help me with the layout and hopefully give me some tips on color for the walls."

The women went inside and Jake squatted in front of the stroller where Zoë lay sleeping. He straightened her jacket and the cap on her head.

Luke watched him. Jake had taken so much abuse from the people in town because of the circumstances of his birth. He'd become hardened, only opening up with his friends. When Jake looked at Zoë, he became a different person, softer, kinder and forgiving. Jake would make sure Zoë would never have to go through what he had suffered as a child.

"I'd better go," Luke said, thinking he was wasting time fooling around with his friends. "Have you guys seen Hank?"

"No," Jake replied, not taking his eyes off Zoë.

"Me, neither," Brady added.

"If you do, give me a call," Luke

shouted on the way to his truck. "See y'all tomorrow night."

He waved as he drove away. His friends stared after him and he knew what they were thinking.

What's going on now?

THE DAY WAS PURE HELL. Henry decided to take over the running of the ranch. Lucy put Luke in charge of looking after his father. Everyone was telling him what to do and he was getting tired of it.

Henry was worried about the heifer auction, so Luke spent the afternoon going over Hank's records. Everything was in order. Hank kept flawless records. The heifers were all tagged and growing fat in a winter coastal pasture waiting for the sale. The cowboys would bring them to the corrals on auction day. Catalogs with a photo of each heifer and her data had been printed for the buyers. Caterers had been booked to serve lunch, and a bar with every liquor imaginable had also been reserved, along with waiters to serve it. There wasn't much left to do, but Henry insisted on going through everything.

By late afternoon, Luke had had enough.

He took his dad back to the house. Henry immediately started listing off what Luke needed to do tomorrow.

"No," Luke said loudly. "You don't have to tell me what I need to do. I know what to do. I've lived and worked here a lot of my life and I'm well acquainted with what goes on. Tomorrow you will stay here and concentrate on your recovery. The therapist is coming and you will do your exercises. In the afternoon, if you want to look at the horses, I'll take you. But otherwise, until Hank returns, I'm running this ranch."

"Now, boy, you listen—"

"That's it, Pa," he cut in. "Take it or leave it."

"Whatever," Henry muttered, slowly making his way to his chair, his cane making loud thuds on the hardwood floor.

"Luke," his mother whispered behind him.

He turned to her. "Mom, I'm not looking for Hank anymore. He'll come home when he wants to."

"Tried to tell her that," Henry mumbled from the den.

"Luke."

"No, Mom. I'm going upstairs."

"But you haven't had dinner."

"I'm not hungry." He took the stairs two at a time, needing to get away, needing to run.

Instead he called Becky.

She could only talk for a minute, but just hearing her calming voice made him feel better.

He lay in bed wondering if there was a way to put this family back together, and if there was a way to have a life in River Bluff.

With Becky.

LUKE WAS DOWN early the next morning. His mom and dad were at the table talking. Or more to the point, arguing. He didn't ask what about. He didn't want to know.

He told Clover he wanted the works for breakfast. After not having any supper, he was starving.

"Mornin'," he said, taking a seat at the table.

Henry gave him a hard stare and his mother looked worried.

"You ready to ride, boy?" Hap asked, nursing a cup of coffee. "Your dad said you're taking over."

"Only until Hank returns." He wrapped

his hands around the warmth of his cup. "Let's be clear on that."

"You sure Hank's coming back?" Henry shot him a look.

"Yeah, Pa, I am." And Luke hoped it was sooner than later.

Hap got to his feet and reached for his hat. "I'll meet you at the bunkhouse."

Nothing else was said and Luke dug into his food. He felt he should apologize, but he didn't know what for. He just didn't like his parents angry with him.

As he placed his hat on his head, he asked Henry, "Do you want to check on the paints this afternoon?"

To Luke's surprise, Henry nodded. "Maybe about three, after the therapist leaves."

Luke spent most of the day in the saddle, something he hadn't done in a while. Hap ran the ranch as flawlessly as Hank. Luke really wasn't needed, but he worked alongside the other cowboys anyway. It was expected of a Chisum.

Later he took his dad to see the paints and he gave Cochise a workout while his dad watched with a gleam in his eye.

Back at the house everything seemed

almost normal, except Hank wasn't there. As a kid he used to think it would be great if Hank left. But he realized it wouldn't be. They were family.

Would Hank ever accept that?

He didn't have time to worry about it.

Tonight was poker night.

CHAPTER ELEVEN

THE GUYS GATHERED at the Circle C in the game room off the garages. Usually when it was Luke's turn to host they played in the meeting room at the barn, but Hank had everything set up for the sale and Luke felt it best to host the boys elsewhere.

And there was an actual poker table in the room. Luke didn't often play in here because the guys liked to horse around and be themselves, and they could do that better in the barn.

His mom knew all the players and always wanted to ask about everyone's families and how they were doing. Lucy didn't understand that poker night was just for the guys. Tonight, with his family facing a crisis, he knew Lucy would keep to the house. Clover had brought the platter of ham, turkey and cheese sandwiches and her homemade kolaches in earlier.

There were ten players tonight. Besides the five friends, Hap and Hardy sat in, as did Harold Knutson, Ed Falconetti and Bill Pinski from the auto-parts store.

"Damn, Luke," Harold said, looking around the room with its small kitchen. "Why haven't we played in here before?"

"Because you make too damn much noise and I don't want to disturb my parents. Let's act like, well, gentlemen, or as close as some of us can get. Remember, no shouting or throwing hamburgers."

"That was an accident," Harold said. "I was upset with Sally."

"Yeah, right." Luke shuffled the cards.

"How is Henry?" Bill asked, taking a seat at the table.

"He's doing better and better," Luke replied

Better than the rest of the Chisum family.

The guys took their seats and the playing got serious. Luke had a hard time concentrating—a first for him. Even in Iraq he could get lost in a poker game, trying to beat the odds, trying to be a winner.

Tonight, though, he kept glancing at his watch. It was after eight, so Becky was home. How long did it take her to fix supper and get the kid to bed? One hour? Two hours? Maybe if the game ended early enough he could ride over and they could talk.

"Luke."

He glanced at Cole. "What?"

"We're playing poker in case you've forgotten. It's your turn to bet or do something. If you're bluffing, it's not working. It's annoying."

Luke made a face at him, and then took a look at the flop—a two of diamonds, a ten of hearts and a seven of spades. He tried to remember what cards he had under his dog tags and realized he had a lousy hand. He'd been getting lousy hands all night. His heart wasn't in playing—too many other distractions.

"I'm out." He leaned back, his hands behind his head, and watched Brady, Cole and Blake battle it out for the pot. The sound of cards shuffling and chips clicking filled the room. The others sat around eating and drinking, but their eyes were on the last three players in the game.

When Brady called, Luke leaned forward and showed the turn card, a two of spades, and another round of betting ensued.

Blake placed a bet.

Brady cursed and folded.

Cole twisted the tooled silver and turquoise money clip that had belonged to his father. He adjusted his baseball cap, studying the cards, and suddenly went all in.

Blake twirled his lucky silver dollar between his fingers and called.

Cole flipped over his hole cards—two jacks.

Blake revealed his cards—a king and a queen.

The guys stood and waited.

Luke turned up the river card—a queen of diamonds.

"Dammit," Cole said.

Blake stood and raised his arms in victory. "Yes."

Luke divvied up the money and the guys sat around talking and finishing off the sandwiches and kolaches. A few more minutes, Luke kept thinking. A few more minutes and he could be out of here and on his way to Becky's.

BECKY PUT THE LAST DISH in the dishwasher and turned it on, glancing at the kitchen clock. Maybe, just maybe, the game was over. She hurried to Shane's room. He was in bed talking on his cell phone, which he tried to hide from her when she knocked and opened the door.

She held out her hand for the phone.

With a deep frown, he placed it in her palm.

"You know the rules—no talking after ten o'clock."

"Jeez, Mom, I'm not a baby." He slumped down in the bed. "I'll be sixteen years old and other kids talk on the phone all they want and whenever they want."

"They're not my kid. My kid obeys the rules or gets his phone taken away."

"Ah, jeez." He turned his back to her. "You're not fair. You're never fair. Brad and I were just talking about our homework and how hard it was."

She felt a moment of remorse for being too strict, but as a single parent she had to be or Shane would never learn discipline. It wasn't easy being the bad guy.

"Apologize and I'll let you have your phone in the morning."

He lay with his back to her and she thought he wasn't going to take the bait. Suddenly he flipped over. "My phone rang and I didn't even look at the time. I just answered it so I don't see why I should apologize for that."

She gave her best hurt-mother expression she'd perfected over the years. "If that's the way you feel." She turned toward the door.

"Okay. Okay. I'm sorry."

She looked straight at him. "What are you sorry for? And don't say it's for using the phone when you're not supposed to. We both know it's much more than that."

"Yes, ma'am." He looked down. "I'm sorry for talking back."

Forcing herself not to sigh with relief, she said, "Turning sixteen doesn't give you the right to be rude to me or to anyone else for that matter. Getting older only gives you more responsibility and I hope you learn to handle it better than with disrespectful behavior."

"Yes, ma'am."

She walked over and pushed his hair from his forehead. "I'm stern for a reason—to guide you into adulthood the only way I know how—by learning discipline and respect." She kissed his forehead. "'Night, son."

"I'm sorry, Mom," he said as she closed the door.

She felt like a hypocrite because someday soon she knew she would be asking for his forgiveness. And she only prayed she was adult enough to handle his response.

This was it—she had to talk to Luke tonight. She couldn't keep her secret one minute longer. Even though hell waited for her, there was no turning back.

Her dad was in the den in his recliner, flipping through a truck magazine. He glanced up as she slipped into her jacket.

"Are you going somewhere?"

"I have to tell Luke tonight. I just can't let this go on any longer." She reached for her purse. "I thought we could get to know each other again and it would soften the blow, but once again, I'm thinking about myself instead of Shane and Luke."

"Rebecca." He put down his magazine. "Why the rush all of a sudden?"

She blinked back a tear. "I'm a stern disciplinarian to Shane when I should be begging him to forgive me for taking so much away from him."

"Rebecca." Hub got to his feet. "The boy has Chisum blood, so you have to be stern or he'll be trying to fly cars off cliffs. He has to have guidance and you have nothing to be sorry for. You did the best you could and I dare anyone to say differently."

"Thanks, Daddy, but your little girl is in the wrong this time. And as much as it's going to hurt, I have to make it right." She handed him Shane's phone. "I took this away from him for talking after hours. He can have it back in the morning." She headed for the back door. "Don't wait up for me."

"Rebecca."

Becky kept walking. She couldn't let her dad talk her out of this.

The lights were on at the Chisums', so she knew Lucy and Henry were still up. Lucy opened the door and didn't seem surprised to see her.

"Oh, Becky, good," Lucy said, waving Becky inside. "I'm glad you're here. Please take Henry's blood pressure. I think it's high again. I don't trust that digital thing."

"Sure." Becky walked into the den. "Hi, Henry."

"I'm fine, Becky. Don't worry with me."

She made a face. "Now you're hurting my feelings."

He smiled, or as close as Henry would ever get to a smile.

Becky opened a box and pulled out a stethoscope and a blood-pressure cuff, then went to work. After a minute, she removed the stethoscope from her ears. "It's a little high, but not in a danger zone. I think you just need some rest."

"I told you, Lu," Henry said. "You worry too much."

"Where's Luke?" Becky asked, putting everything back into the box.

Lucy waved a hand toward the garages. "He's in the game room playing poker with his friends."

Knowing the Wild Bunch, they'd probably play until after midnight. Damn. She needed to talk to Luke tonight.

No one seemed in a hurry to leave. They were razzing each other, but mostly they seemed to be razzing Luke. And he'd done enough crazy things to keep them going for a while.

"Remember that time you boys were working on that '66 Ford pickup," Bill asked. "Y'all planned to race it somewhere."

"Yeah," Jake said. "It took a lot of our summer evenings."

"Y'all needed spark plugs and didn't have money to buy 'em so you guys dared Luke to steal 'em from my store."

"Damn, Bill, never knew you were aware of that." Brady gathered all the chips.

"Yeah. Luke managed to steal those plugs without me noticing, but the next day he came in and paid for 'em." Bill grinned. "Bet you guys didn't know that."

The friends glanced at each other. "No, we didn't," Jake finally said.

"Where did you get the money?" Cole asked.

"Sold the watch my parents gave me for my birthday," Luke replied.

"What made you do that?" Blake was curious.

"I just kept thinking about ol' Bill sweating out a living in that parts store and I knew I had to find a way to pay for the plugs." Luke handed Brady the cards to put in the silver box.

Bill leaned in close and whispered, "Wanna hear a secret? I got paid four times for those plugs."

The friends exchanged more glances and laughter filled their eyes as they realized they'd been had.

Cole shrugged. "I washed cars at my mother's church and gave the money to Bill."

"I sold that expensive baseball glove Dad gave me," Brady admitted.

"I slipped money out of Uncle Verne's wallet when he was stone drunk." Jake came clean. "Didn't figure he'd miss it and he hadn't paid me an allowance for helping in the bar for weeks." Jake rubbed his jaw. "Makes me wonder why Bill kept it a secret all these years and why we never told each other."

"We're the Wild Bunch," Luke responded. "We couldn't destroy our image."

"You son of a bitch." Brady pointed a finger at Bill. "You took money from teenage boys."

"Teenage boys who steal." Bill took up for himself. "I thought it would be a good learning experience for you boys."

Luke got to his feet. "You know what, boys? Let's take ol' Bill down to the cow trough and give him a dunking. It'll be a good learning experience, don't you think?"

"I'm in," Brady said.

"Me, too," Cole and Jake said in unison.

"You have to catch me first." Bill made a dive for the door. Brady blocked it and

Bill ran around the table with Luke, Jake and Cole after him. Hoots of laughter and curses filled the room.

Suddenly the door was flung open and Hank stood there. Everyone froze in place and stared at his haggard appearance. With a growth of beard and bloodshot eyes, Hank looked as if he'd been ridden hard and put up wet.

He scowled at the men in the room. "What's going on here?"

Luke walked to the table. "It's poker night. Want to join us?"

His scowled deepened. "When in the hell are you going to grow up? There's more to life than playing poker."

"We'd better go," Blake said.

"No," Luke shouted. "This is my home, too, and I have a right to have friends over."

"You have a right to be responsible, but I don't see much of that." Hank spat the words at him. "You get half this ranch handed to you on a platter, but what have you done to earn it?"

Luke had about had his fill of Hank and his mouth. He reached for the cards in the silver box. He knew of a way to put an end to this once and for all.

"Tell you what, Hank." He sat down and shuffled the cards. "I'll play you for my half of the ranch."

"You're an idiot, Luke," Hank snarled.

He kept shuffling. No one else moved or said a word. "I'll make it easy for you," Luke went on. "If you win, I'll sign over my half to you. If I win, you'll get off my back for the rest of my life."

"Luke," Brady said under his breath. "What are you doing?"

"See, Hank, my friends are worried about me. I'm not known for making great decisions." He set the cards in front of him. "What's it going to be?"

Hank glared at him.

"Shut up or play," Luke said, and stared straight back.

"Luke." This time it was Jake, but Luke ignored him.

Hank still didn't move.

"Luke." Blake touched his shoulder, but he didn't respond.

His eyes and attention were on his brother. "You want this ranch? Here's your chance. A good old-fashioned Texas Hold 'Em poker game." He scooted forward in his chair. "And I'll even make it easier for you in case you don't have the guts. One hand, no playing or betting. The luck of the draw and the winner takes all. A Texas bluff kind of playing."

"An idiot kind of playing," was Hank's response, but he pulled out a chair and slumped into it.

"Brady'll be the dealer," Luke said.

Brady held up his hands and backed away. "Nope, not me."

"Cole."

Cole shook his head, as did Jake.

"This is insane," Blake told him. "Stop this."

His friends didn't understand and he didn't have time to explain it to them. This was the only way to restore some sanity to his family. Out of the corner of his eye, he saw Hap slip out the door. He didn't want any part of Luke's kind of Texas bluff and Luke didn't blame him.

"I'll do it," Knut said and sat down.

"You bastard," Cole hissed. For Cole to speak up, Luke knew he was upset. But nothing was going to change Luke's mind, not even his friends.

Silence filled the room as Harold shuffled. The only sound was the cards slapping together. Knut dealt two hole cards to Luke and then to Hank. He laid the three flop cards on the table, faceup. The turn and river card were facedown.

Everyone stared at the flop—two of spades, four of hearts and a nine of diamonds. Luke glanced at his hole cards and then laid them on the table for everyone to see: four of spades and a three of hearts. He had a pair of fours so far. Not good, but not bad.

Hank turned up his two cards—a ten of diamonds and a king of hearts.

No one spoke and Luke nodded to Harold. He flipped the turn card faceup— a six of spades.

The men gathered closer around the table. Luke nodded again and Knut turned the river card faceup—a king of diamonds.

Hank won with a pair of kings.

Luke stood and raised his hands. "You win, big brother, fair and square. This ranch is yours."

Hank stood in an angry thrust and his chair went flying backward, clattering against the tiled floor. "You think so much of this ranch that you'd bet it in a stupid game of poker?"

Each word was like the slash of a blade across Luke's chest. He'd taken so much from his brother and he didn't know how much more he could stomach. Luke had used the poker game as a way to settle the ranch problem once and for all. All his hands tonight had been lousy and he knew once he was in that slump he stayed there. He'd been right, but it seemed there was no pleasing Hank.

"This isn't just about land, Luke," Hank railed on. "It's about blood, too. Father-and-son blood. This land comes to me first because I'm blood. Do you even understand that?"

"Yes, I understand I'm not blood and this ranch is yours. Now it is, so stop your bellyaching."

"Are you just plumb stupid, or what?" Hank's bloodshot eyes seemed to bulge out of his head and the stench of alcohol was strong on his breath.

Luke took a deep breath and vaguely noticed that Cole and Blake had slipped out the door. "I'm going to let that pass because you're drunk off your ass."

"I should have the right to hand this ranch

down to my son," Hank shouted the words so loudly that Luke felt them ringing in his ears.

Son? What the hell was Hank talking about? He didn't have a son. He had a daughter. Wait. Hank had been married before. It had lasted about six months. Could the woman have been pregnant when she'd left? No. Their parents would have known about it, so what was Hank talking about?

"You don't have a son," Luke reminded him.

"Goddammit, I have a son." Hank pounded his fist on the table. Everyone jumped back, except Luke. "Dad promised I could give my son this ranch when the time came. He promised I'd inherit the ranch and I could pass it on to my son. Henry Chisum broke his word."

Luke couldn't make sense of any of this, so he decided to force the issue. "Where is this son?"

"I'm looking at him."

"What?" Luke felt the blood drain from his face.

"I became a father at sixteen and gave up all rights to you on the condition you stayed in the Chisum family." Hank took a ragged breath. "I agreed to stay out of your life on the condition that when you were older I would be the one to tell you the truth. The ranch would be passed down from generation to generation. That was the agreement."

Hank was drunk. Why was he spouting such nonsense?

Luke glanced up and saw Becky and his mom standing in the doorway, Cole and Blake behind them. Becky looked concerned, his mom worried.

In that instant he knew the unbelievable truth.

I'm Hank's son.

CHAPTER TWELVE

THROUGH THE TURMOIL of his mind, Luke heard the whirl of the helicopter blades, felt the aircraft wobble as fuel fumes filled his lungs and the medic's screams echoed in his ears.

He was going down into that black hole again. His body was being jarred from the impact and he tried to stay focused. He tried to breathe, but the blackness coated his skin, his thoughts.

This time he would not survive.

But he held on with more strength than he thought he possessed. His arms ached; his chest burned. He had to get out, though. He had to get out now. To survive he had to act quickly.

He spun toward the door and ran.

"Luke," Becky screamed, but he kept running. Not even her voice could stop him.

He ran and ran through the darkness, his

chest heaving, until he hit a barbed-wire fence. It caught him like a rabbit in a snare. The barbs cut into his chest, his arms. He fought wildly until he was free, then he was over the fence and off again, feeling his way through brush and trees.

Suddenly he stumbled off a craggy ledge and catapulted to the bottom of a ravine, where he lay on the cold, hard rock. His lungs burned and he struggled to catch his breath.

He had to keep moving.

Rolling to his feet, he trudged on. The enemy was behind him and the only way to survive was to keep running, to find shelter and safety. His foot caught on a tree root and he toppled into the tall grasses. His energy was spent, his breathing labored. He lifted his head and saw the moonlight reflecting off the pond.

His and Becky's pond.

He crawled on all fours to the oak tree and dragged himself up against it. Wincing at the pain in his body, he wiped at his face and felt the wetness. He gulped in air and let the tears flow. There wasn't any way to stop them.

Nor was there any way to end this nightmare.

"I'LL GET THE HORSES," Hap said. "We'll find him."

"I'm right behind you." Brady was at the door.

"Me, too." Jake grabbed his leather jacket.

"Let me call Tessa and I'll be right with y'all." Cole pushed a button on his phone.

"The same for me," Blake added, the phone to his ear.

"No." Becky shook her head. "Luke needs some time and we're going to give it to him."

"But, Bec…"

"No, Brady." She remained firm. "Luke doesn't want to talk to anyone, except maybe me, so I'm going alone." She looked at Hap. "Please bring the Polaris Ranger to the house. I'll go in it."

"Hardy will bring it around."

"Thank you, Becky." Lucy wiped away tears.

Becky didn't have anything left to say. She was numb. Hank sat in a chair, his head buried in his hands.

Lucy touched his shoulder. "Let's go into the house, son. We have to tell your father."

Hank stood, his shoulders bowed, his face etched in pain. "Mom…"

"I know." No recriminations, no judgment—enough of that had been said to last a lifetime. They didn't need to rehash it tonight.

Becky turned to Cole. "Is there any bottled water in the fridge?"

"I think I saw some in there. I'll get it."

There was one ham sandwich left on the tray and Becky wrapped it in a couple of paper towels. Cole brought a box with several bottles of water and Hap slipped a bottle of Jack Daniel's inside.

"He might need that more than anything."

A horn honked.

"That's Hardy with the Ranger," Hap said. "You sure you don't want me to go with you?"

"Thanks, Hap, but I have to do this alone." She knew that was the way Luke would want it.

"Be sure you have your cell phone," Blake instructed. "And call if you need anything. We'll all be waiting."

"Go home to Annie," Becky told him. "Everyone go home. Luke will need your support tomorrow."

"God." Jake ran a hand through his hair.

"Who would have ever thought that Hank was Luke's father?"

"That's a blow." Brady shook his head. "And with Harold here it's going to be all over town tomorrow."

"We can't stop that," Blake said. "But we can be here for Luke."

Becky hurried to the ATV and the guys followed her. Cole placed the box in the back.

"It's awful dark out here." Brady glanced toward the sky. "Are you sure you don't want some company?"

Becky climbed into the Ranger. "Don't use the poor-little-woman routine on me, Jock Man. I can do anything you can do."

"And probably better," Jake teased.

The vehicle was running, so Becky shifted into gear. "Go home," she shouted as she headed for the cattle guard.

BECKY DROVE THROUGH the darkness, the headlights guiding her. Every now and then she'd stop, kill the motor and shout Luke's name.

The rustle of the wind, the chirp of crickets and an unbelievable quiet answered her frantic calls. The darkness wrapped around her and she began to despair of ever finding him. Then she thought of the pond. She turned off the road, trying to gauge how far away it was, but in the dark it was difficult. She'd often thought that she could find her way there blindfolded.

That had been from her house, though. It was totally different coming from Great Oaks. And traveling off the road was dangerous. She didn't want to drive into a rocky crevice. She turned again and the headlights caught the pond, the light glistening across its smooth surface with an eerie, misty feel, like something out of a horror movie.

Then she saw him.

Luke was sitting against the oak tree and he looked bloody.

OhmyGod!

She slammed on the brakes, jumped out and ran to him, falling down at his side. "Luke."

He didn't respond. He just stared off to the pond with a blank expression. His face was scratched and bloody; his shirt was ripped in places and soaked with more blood.

She gently touched his face. "Luke."

No response. He was almost comatose.

What had happened to him?

She ran to the Ranger and found a flashlight under the seat. Flipping on the light, she turned off the vehicle. She needed something to clean his wounds. Opening the toolbox in the back, she found paper towels. Great. She grabbed the bottled water and sprinted to him once again.

Laying the flashlight on the ground, she knelt at his side and twisted off the cap on the bottle. She placed it to his dry lips, spilling some water on them. She did that a couple of times before he licked it away with his tongue.

"Luke. Oh, Luke. Please drink some water."

He moaned a sound that tore at her heart. It reminded her of a sound a wounded animal made after being caught in a vicious trap.

She put the bottle to his lips and he took a swallow.

"Luke."

"Bec…"

"Yes, it's me." She poured water on a paper towel and dabbed at the blood on his face.

"Am… Am I dead?"

Her breath caught in her throat. "No," she managed to say.

"I...I should be."

She did the only thing she could. She wrapped her arms around him. "Oh, Luke. I'm so, so sorry."

He rubbed his face in the curve of her neck and she felt his tears and his blood as it soaked her blouse. They stayed that way, locked together, holding on to something that was real. But her nurse's instinct intruded. His wounds needed tending.

She drew back. "Let me clean your wounds." She poured more water on the towel and started to clean his face. She picked up the light to take a closer look. The scratches were on the surface and not deep. That was good.

After placing the light on the ground, she began to unbutton his shirt, then peeled it away from his damp body. He winced but didn't say anything. With the light, she looked at the wounds on his chest and arms. The ones on his chest were deeper.

"How did you do this?"

"Barbed wire."

She meticulously cleaned every cut. "You'll need a tetanus shot."

"Had one last month. Hank insisted I..."

He heaved an agonizing breath. "Hank is my father. How can that be?"

She sank back on her heels. "You have to come back and talk to him and to your parents."

He shook his head. "No. I'm not ready to do that."

"Luke…"

He reached for her hand and linked his fingers with hers. "So many times in my dreams I relive the crash in Iraq. I can feel every awkward movement of the hit helicopter, smell the fuel and sense that fall into nothing. That fall is broken only by the screams of the medic and the wounded soldier's cries. I have to land the copter to save them—to save myself." He gulped a breath. "Tonight I was going down once again into that emptiness, that darkness. I had to run to save myself. When I hit the fence, I fought even harder. But nothing is going to save me from this. Nothing."

"Talking will," she told him, squeezing his fingers. "The truth will."

"They lied to me, Bec. All these years they lied to me."

"They had their reasons."

She was defending the Chisums, but she

was also defending herself. There was no way to justify her secret now. It would destroy him.

"I wonder who she was," he said matter-of-factly.

"Who?"

"My mother."

She swallowed. "Probably a girl Hank knew in high school."

Just like us.

"I wonder where she is."

She raised their clasped hands and kissed his knuckles. "Let's go back to Great Oaks and Hank will answer all your questions and I can treat your wounds properly."

He released her hand, slid his arm around her waist and pulled her next to him. She rested her head on his shoulder.

"Do you remember all the times we came here as teenagers?" he asked.

"Yes. It was the halfway point for both of us."

"We carved our initials in this tree and they're still there. I checked when I came home from Walter Reed."

She had checked it many times herself and wondered how so much love could get lost in the struggles of life.

"I'm sorry I hurt you," he said, his voice as sincere as she'd ever heard it.

"And I'm sorry I wouldn't listen."

"How did we go so wrong, Becky?"

She drew back, needing to see his face in the glow of the flashlight. "It was my fault."

"Bec…"

"It was," she insisted. "I was this shy, insecure girl whose father was the sheriff and all the boys feared him. Then Luke Chisum asked me for a date. I felt like a princess and all my insecurities seemed to melt away. When Rachel told me about the dare, I just couldn't get over the fact that you were laughing behind my back with your poker buddies. I couldn't get beyond that pain, that humiliation."

"Bec…"

"I know the truth now and I'll always regret what I put us through."

"How could you marry someone else? How could you?" His voice broke on the last word and she wrapped her arms around him.

"I never loved Danny the way I loved you. I'll never love anyone the way I loved you." She framed his face and kissed him with everything she was feeling. It might be wrong, like so many decisions in her life. But it felt right.

He was hurting and she knew how to stop his pain.

"Oh, Bec." He took her lips with a fiery passion fueled by the events of the night. She tasted his tongue and moaned as his hands found those special places that drove her wild. One by one he undid the buttons on her blouse and slipped it from her shoulders. His lips blazed a path to her shoulder, to her chest and her cleavage. Deftly he unsnapped her bra and her breasts spilled into his hands. He nibbled and teased until she gripped his head with total pleasure. It had been so long since he'd touched her this way that she couldn't get enough.

He raised his head, and her hands spanned his shoulders then trailed down his chest through the tiny swirls of hair. He was more muscled, more mature and that sparked her desire over the top. She quickly undid his belt and the snap on his jeans.

"Wait," he said as he bent to remove his boots. They shimmied out of their clothes within seconds and then they were skin on skin and everything fit just like before—

hips on pelvis, hard against soft. It had never felt more erotic.

He eased to the side as his hand caressed her curves and rested on her stomach, then teased the triangle between her legs. His lips followed with mind-blowing sensations that stimulated every part of her.

She reached for him then, feeling his length and fullness and needing him now more than she ever had. "Luke," she moaned, stroking him.

He gasped and reached for his jeans.

"What… What are you doing?" She lifted her head.

"Condom," he muttered, opening his wallet.

She smiled, remembering all those times he'd frantically searched for condoms. That alone should have brought her to her senses, but it just aroused her more.

As he sheathed himself, she said, "You still carry condoms?"

"Whenever you gave in, I wanted to be ready."

She laughed, a bubbly sound that floated away through the darkness. Luke lay beside her, kissing her deep and long, and she forgot everything but him and this moment.

The moment of loving Luke again.

When she'd reached that point of no return, she moaned, "Luke, please."

He slid between her legs and thrust into her with one strong plunge. She wrapped her legs around him, guiding him deeper and deeper inside her. His lips covered hers and her arms locked behind his neck as they renewed an old dance their bodies knew well. Each touch, each thrust brought them closer to that pinnacle they both desired.

"Luke," she groaned his name as she reached the apex of bone-melting ecstasy a moment before he did.

He shuddered against her and she held on to every last second of pleasure, wondering how she'd lived all these years without him, without this fulfillment only he could give her.

They lay bound together for a second longer. Luke rolled to the side and gathered her close. Her body was almost liquid from what she'd just experienced.

"Oh, sweet Becky Lynn," Luke whispered against her skin.

"I should be taking care of your wounds." She touched his face, her fingers lingering over the roughness of his jaw.

"Oh, you have, believe me. I'm all better now." Laughter filled his voice, so different from the despair of an hour ago.

She lay in the grass, staring up at the majestic cathedral of the sky and all its brilliant lights. Her hand curled into a fist as all the doubts returned. Was there a way to save their relationship, this magic that had always been between them?

There was only one way—the truth.

He kissed her lips. "What are you thinking?"

She ran her fingers through his hair. "That we need to talk."

"Not tonight, Bec."

The pain was returning. She'd heard it in his voice. She pulled him to her, holding on to this moment in time—holding on because tomorrow the truth would rip their worlds apart.

And for them there might not be another moment like this.

CHAPTER THIRTEEN

THE HEAT FROM their bodies kept them warm, but after a while they became aware of the chilly March night. Luke gathered their clothes and they quickly dressed. He paused over his tattered and bloody shirt.

Becky examined it. "This is a mess. Your jeans are torn, too."

"I don't care."

"Wait a minute." She whirled toward the Ranger. "I saw something in the toolbox."

"Bec…"

"I'll be right back."

In the toolbox she found the chambray shirt she'd seen earlier. It probably belonged to one of the cowboys. She carried it back to him and held it up.

"Don't know how clean it is, but it's better than your shirt. Try it on for size."

He muttered something she didn't catch, but slipped his arms into the sleeves.

Buttoning it, her hands lingered over his chest. "Much better."

He pulled her close and she held on again, knowing the worst was yet to come. "Let's go to Great Oaks," she said into his chest.

As he remained silent, she glanced up.

"I'm not ready." He smoothed her hair from her face. "Please understand that."

"I do, but I'm worried about your cuts. They need to be treated."

"You've treated them in the best way possible."

She knew he was grinning and she reached up to feel his face.

"You gave me hope and I needed that, but now I need time to sort through my thoughts, my life." He kissed the tip of her nose. "I'll be back tomorrow or the next day."

"Where will you go?"

"The Circle C is a big place and I know every inch of it. I'll be fine communing with nature."

"Oh." She knew she had to give him this time, but it wasn't easy.

He pulled her down to the ground to sit under the tree. She leaned against him, listening to the beat of his heart as the crickets serenaded them and an owl hooted in a nearby tree. Coyotes howled in the distance, but Becky felt safe locked in Luke's arms.

But she couldn't stay much longer. Her son was waiting.

Our son.

She'd never felt the pain of that more than she did at that moment. Kissing the column of his neck, she said, "I have to go."

"I love you." He turned his head and gave her a long and lingering kiss.

She breathed in the musky scent of his skin and sweet desire filled her once again. Those special words hovered on her lips, but she couldn't say them. They were tangled in secrets and deceit, and if she said them the truth would come pouring out.

And tonight, Luke couldn't handle any more truth.

She rose to her feet and walked to the Ranger for the box of food. Setting it on the ground beside him, she said, "There's water, a ham sandwich and a pint of liquor."

"Thanks."

"Luke."

"Go home, Becky, and let me deal with what's left of my life."

Her heart contracted. "If you're not back by tomorrow, I'll come looking for you."

"I'll look forward to it."

That sounded like the old Luke and she knew he was going to be okay. He just needed time. Her feet were rooted to the ground and she couldn't make herself move. She was just so worried about him.

"You don't want those cuts to get infected." Now she sounded like his mother.

She could feel him gazing at her through the moonlight. "I'll be fine. I've lived through worse. Go home and I'll talk to you soon. Okay?"

"Okay."

This time her feet moved and she made her way to the Ranger. As she drove away, tears trailed down her cheeks. She swerved to miss a raccoon, but she steadily kept driving toward Great Oaks, refusing to look back.

As she crossed the cattle guard, she saw Hank pacing by the garages under the flood of the spotlights used to scare away coyotes. She parked by her Tahoe and he immediately strolled to her side. Hap appeared out of the shadows but he didn't move toward her.

"Did you find Luke?" Hank asked.

"Yes." She climbed out of the Ranger.

"Where is he? Why didn't he come back with you?"

"He said he needed time and I had to respect his wishes."

"What the hell for? He doesn't know what he's doing."

She sighed in frustration. "And, evidently, neither do you."

His face hardened into a mask of stone. "This is none of your business."

"Then I'm going home." She headed for her car.

"Wait."

She paused, wondering if Hank was completely devoid of emotions.

"What did he say?"

She turned. "I just told you. He's hurt and confused and has to sort through all that before he can see anyone."

"But he's talking to you?"

"Yes."

He reached toward her hair and pulled a blade of grass from it. "Is that all he did?"

Looking him square in the eye, she said, "If I were you, Hank, I wouldn't be so judgmental. And you might practice the words *I'm sorry* until you can say them with some degree of emotion." She opened her door. "Tell Lucy that Luke is fine and I'll call her tomorrow."

"Becky, wait."

But she'd had enough. She started her engine and blocked out his words.

WHEN SHE ENTERED HER HOUSE, everything was quiet and dark except for the kitchen light her dad had left on for her. She went to her room and stripped, slipping on a T-shirt. She wanted a shower, but that would have to wait until the morning. The running water would wake her father.

Slipping under the covers, she stared at the clock—3:00 a.m. God, she had three hours to sleep before she had to get up.

She wrapped her arms around her waist and let herself get lost in the memory of Luke's touch and Luke's love. Her skin tingled with awareness, that feeling of being alive and whole and experiencing every nuance of what that meant.

But how long would this feeling last?

She flipped over, feeling disgusted with herself and her weakness. She'd told Hank not to judge others and she could apply that to herself. The reason she couldn't say she loved Luke was that the words were tainted with deception.

She wasn't worthy of his love.

Oh, how she hated that expression and she hated that poor, pitiful-me feeling. She was worthy of love just like every woman. She wasn't a saint. She had faults and she prayed Luke would recognize that.

This time, she wasn't giving up and walking away.

She was fighting for their love.

Until there was no reason left to fight.

THE NEXT MORNING, the ringing of the phone woke Becky. She pushed herself up in bed, trying to pry her eyes open as she reached for the handset. It was Annie and Blake, wanting news of Luke. As soon as she replaced the receiver, the phone rang again. This time it was Brady. She told him Luke was fine and to pass the word. But she didn't even make it to the bathroom before Jake and Cole called.

She assured everyone that Luke just needed time and would be back soon. After a quick shower, she dressed and headed for the kitchen, needing coffee. Her dad sat at the table, reading the paper.

When he saw her, he folded the paper and laid it down. "From the way you look this morning, I guess it didn't go well last night?"

As she poured a cup of coffee, she heard the anxiety in his voice and realized she should have called him. She quickly told him what had happened.

His shaggy eyebrows shot up. "What! Hank is Luke's father?"

"So it seems." She leaned against the cabinet, sipping on the hot liquid.

"Holy crap!"

"I never had a chance to tell him, and now he's hurting so much I don't think I'll ever be able to do it. It's going to kill him."

"Still…"

"I know, Daddy. I know."

"Rebecca."

"I'll be fine." She headed for the hall. "I have to get Shane up for school."

She didn't want to rehash that old subject. There was only one option and now she had to find the courage to just do it.

TOWARD DAWN, LUKE ATE the sandwich and drank a bottle of water. As a pearly gray light crept over the landscape, he got to his feet, wincing as pain shot through every bone in his body. He opened the whiskey and took a large swallow. It burned his throat as it went down. He coughed and took another swallow.

After it flowed through his system like a fiery arrow, he tied his bloody shirt around his waist and made a pouch for the liquor and the water. Then he started walking. Two hours later, he reached the deepest south section of the ranch, the land Hank leased to deer hunters. The cabin on the Medina River was the campsite, but since deer season had ended in January, the cabin was empty.

The cabin stood on blocks because the river flooded in this low part. He found the hidden key, opened the door and went in. A musty, mildewy smell greeted him. There were two bedrooms which could each sleep four people on each side of the large den and kitchen. Everything here was primitive; electricity came from a generator and water from a windmill.

This was what men from the city called *roughing it,* and they paid big bucks to do so.

He headed for a bedroom and fell across a mattress. The hunters supplied their own sheets. Luke didn't need sheets, though. All he needed was rest and the taste of Jack Daniel's.

He reached for the whiskey and took

several swigs. He set the bottle on the floor, then fell asleep.

When he awoke, it was late evening. He winced as he crawled out of bed and the scratches on his body stung as if bees had attacked him. Stumbling into the den, he realized he was hungry. He searched the cupboards: beef jerky, cans of beans and more liquor.

It was just what he needed to fade into oblivion. Or to doctor his wounds. He decided on the latter. After removing his pouch and shirt, he grabbed some paper towels and poured Jack Daniel's over them. Then he dabbed at his scratches. As soon as the liquor soaked into the wounds, his body felt on fire.

"Damn. Damn. Damn." He jumped around, fanning his chest. After a moment the burning stopped.

Becky would be proud of him, he thought. *Becky*. She was the only thing holding him together.

He grabbed the jerky, a can of beans and a can opener, then went outside and sat on the step. Watching the easy-flowing Medina River, he ate his meal. The jerky was salty and made him thirsty. He'd drunk all his water. Glancing to his right, he saw the ancient windmill turning in the breeze. A cistern and a cow trough were beside it.

He went inside for something to carry water in. A small bucket was all he could find and all he needed. After tinkering with the windmill, it didn't take him long to have plenty of water.

Sitting at the edge of the river, he drank his fill. Suddenly he heard the whine of a motor. Was it Becky? His heart kicked into high gear.

A four wheeler came into sight. It wasn't Becky. It was her kid. Shane gunned the motor as he zoomed over small rocks, spinning the wheeler then going back and starting over again. What was the kid doing out here?

A part of the river narrowed between two craggy ledges. There was maybe sixty feet between them. The kid stood, leaned over the motor and aimed the wheeler toward the ledge. He held down the throttle, zooming at a breakneck speed across the ledge to the end that fell into the Medina River.

Luke stood. What the hell was the kid doing?

As Shane reached the end of the ledge, he

spun the wheeler away and headed back. He stopped and then revved the motor, getting ready for another run.

That crazy kid. He was planning on jumping from one ledge to the other. Luke hurried toward him.

Standing, the boy kept gunning the motor, and then he saw Luke. His eyes opened wide and he sank into the seat.

Luke motioned to the wheeler. "Kill it."

The boy turned off the engine.

"What do you think you're doing?"

The kid shrugged. "Nothin'."

"Like hell." Luke glanced to the ledges. "You were thinking of flying this thing—" he kicked the wheel "—across to the other side."

"Maybe. What's it to you?"

The kid had guts. He'd give him that.

"You're on Chisum land and you're trespassing. That's what it is to me."

"The deer hunters are gone and this is a cool place to ride. I wasn't hurting anything."

"Does your mother know you're here?"

The boy glanced down and Luke had his answer.

"Go home, kid, and if I catch you out here

again doing stupid stuff, I'll tell your mother."

"I didn't figure you for a snitch."

"Go home, kid."

"My name is Shane." His chest puffed out.

"Go home, Shane." He dragged out the last word.

Shane looked him over. "What happened to you?"

"Nothing," he muttered and walked away.

The kid had the audacity to follow. Luke resumed his spot in the grass by the river and Shane plopped down beside him.

"Did you get into a fight?"

Luke didn't answer.

"Because you look like you did and you look like you lost."

Luke glared at him. "Do you not understand the meaning of the words *go home?*"

"You're kind of grouchy."

Luke sighed and watched the lazy movement of the water, saying nothing. Luke thought if he ignored the kid long enough, he'd go away.

"What's it like to fly a Black Hawk?"

Luke remained quiet.

"I'd like to join the army, but my mom,

dad and grandpa want me to go to college. I like action, though. Did you get to fire at the enemy?"

Luke turned his gaze to Shane. His career as a soldier had been the most honorable thing he'd ever done. It had also been the most horrific. For Becky, he had to discourage Shane. "My mission was to retrieve wounded soldiers from behind enemy lines and fly them to field hospitals to receive aid."

"That's cool."

"There's nothing cool about war, kid. Most of the soldiers I retrieved were in so much pain they were screaming for their mamas or begging for someone to end their misery."

Shane swallowed and his expression changed.

"But you helped them, didn't you? You received the Purple Heart."

"And I'd give it back in a heartbeat if every one of those guys had made it home to their mamas alive, but some came home in a pine box."

Shane swallowed again.

"There's nothing cool about war, guns and senseless dying. I left here an eighteen-year-old kid thinking I could do anything and everything I wanted. But I'm telling you, stay in school and please your mom, because growing up on a battlefield sucks the life right out of you and makes you old before your time."

The kid didn't have a comeback.

"Go to college, have fun, enjoy the parties and enjoy the girls. Just enjoy life the way young people are supposed to. Growing up will come fast enough."

Shane plucked at the grass. "I don't understand girls."

God, he didn't want to have this discussion with Danny Howard's son. But he was also Becky's son.

"None of us guys do, kid, so get used to it."

"But these older girls keep coming on to me and I don't know how to handle it."

"How much older?"

"Katie's three years older and Brittany's a year ahead of me."

"I'd definitely ax Katie."

"I already figured that out." Shane picked up a rock and threw it at an armadillo, which quickly scurried away. "I really like Abby, but she gets mad when these other girls make moves on me."

"Well, kid, I'd say you have what is known as a 'no problem.' Let everyone know you like Abby and the other problem will go away. And, trust me—your mom will be very pleased if you stay away from older girls."

"You must really know my mom."

Luke felt a catch in his throat. "Everyone in River Bluff knows Becky."

"Yeah."

"And you'd better get home before she sends out a search party."

Shane stood and brushed dirt from his jeans.

"If I catch you doing anything stupid again, I *will* tell your mom."

"Okay. Are you staying out here?"

"For a little while."

Shane raised a hand in farewell. "Bye, Luke."

Luke watched him as he ran and jumped on the four wheeler, then revved it up. He spun it around and took off flying over the rocks.

"Damn kid," Luke muttered. Talking to him had accomplished nothing. Shane craved speed and Luke knew the feeling.

He rose to his feet and glanced at the

landscape around him. Chisum land. So many times he'd felt he had no right to any part of it. He wasn't a blood Chisum.

He ran his hands over his face. Every time he'd left here, he couldn't wait to get back. In Iraq, he'd dreamed of stepping foot on Circle C soil once again and driving under the live oaks to Great Oaks. That pull Hank had talked about was strong in him and he'd never understood it—until now. This land had been passed down from one Chisum generation to the next. That was blood and it ran through his veins.

He was a Chisum.

A blood Chisum.

Now he had to go home and face his family.

CHAPTER FOURTEEN

"BUT FIRST I NEED A DRINK," Luke said to himself, then walked back to the porch and picked up a bottle of Jim Beam he'd found in the cabinet. He took a long swig, swallowed and made a face as it went down. "Maybe more than one." He tipped up the bottle.

He woke up stretched out on the porch, his head feeling as if someone was tap dancing on it. Damn! He grabbed his head and said another curse word. That didn't help the pain. He managed to sit up and the world did a slow dance all on its own.

Son of a bitch.

After a moment, everything came into focus and he was able to breathe without wincing. He'd been in Afghanistan and Iraq, and not once had he ever gotten this drunk. So much for being grown-up and able to handle the bumps in the road. This one had completely derailed him.

He took a slow breath.

I am Hank Chisum's son.

How long would it take before he could even think that without wanting a drink of liquor?

He heard the horses before he saw them. At first he thought it was the tap dancer in his head, then realized exactly what it was.

Riders.

Hap rode in, pulling the reins of a horse behind him. He dismounted, tied the horses to a limb and strolled over. Cocking back his hat, he gave Luke the once-over.

"Now ain't you a fine sight."

His voice boomed through Luke's head with the force of a foghorn.

Luke winced. "Not so loud, please."

Hap glanced at the liquor bottles on the porch. "You're drunk as a skunk, boy. I thought you had more sense."

"Go away." Luke held his head with both hands.

Hap reached for Luke's arm and jerked him to his feet. For a scrawny guy, Hap's fingers were like steel. Luke was in so much pain that he didn't have the strength to fight back. Hap pulled him to the cistern and opened the tap. Cool water squirted on Luke's head.

He didn't jump back. He held up his face to the water and let it pour over him, its coolness shocking and rejuvenating him. Suddenly the water stopped and Hap handed him a towel. Luke hadn't even realized Hap had left to go into the cabin.

"I brought you breakfast and coffee," Hap said on his way to his horse.

Luke plopped onto the step and dabbed at his body with the towel. Hap handed him something wrapped in tinfoil and a Thermos of coffee. Inside the foil, Luke found soft tacos filled with scrambled eggs and sausage.

"Damn, Hap, this is enough for three people."

"You eat like three people so what's the problem?"

Luke opened the Thermos and guzzled the coffee. "Thanks, Hap. I needed that."

They were both quiet as Luke ate. The only sounds were the birds chirping, the water gurgling and an occasional neighing of the horses.

"How did you find me?" Luke asked as he finished off the tacos.

"Cowboy's instinct."

"Yeah, right. Becky's kid told you."

"That, too." Hap nodded. "I know this has hit you hard, boy, but hiding out and drinking don't help."

"Did you know *he* was my father?"

Hap spit chewing tobacco onto the ground. "Nope. Your parents kept that close to their chests."

"So you don't know who my mother is?"

"Nope. You have to come home to find that out." In a slow movement, Hap rose to his feet. "You ready to ride?"

"This isn't easy."

"I know, boy, but I'll be right there with you, and if you want to get drunk afterward I'll go with you to do that, too."

Luke got to his feet, knowing it was time to face his family. He reached for the reins on the limb and swung onto the bay mare. "Clover hates it when you get drunk."

"What Clover doesn't know won't hurt her one little bit."

Luke felt the power of the horse beneath him and the chill of the morning breeze on his wet clothes. He glanced north. "I'm through drinking for now."

"That's even better," Hap said, swinging into the saddle as he had for sixty years— with ease and comfort. "Let's ride."

Luke kneed his horse and her hooves kicked up dust as he followed Hap toward Great Oaks and home.

AN HOUR LATER THEY RODE into the barn. Luke dismounted and Hap reached for the reins. He nodded toward the house. "Go on. I'll take care of your horse."

Luke took his time strolling to the house. The garages, the house, the backyard were the same, yet different. The old oak tree he'd dived out of with a cape tied around his neck was still there. He'd been smart enough to put an air mattress below. He'd dived three times before his mother had caught him.

But Lucy wasn't his mother.

The basketball hoop and net were still attached to the garage where he, Brady, Cole and Jake horsed around. They bet on everything—who could make a shot, who couldn't, who was going to win, who was going to lose. They'd never bet, though, that Hank was Luke's father. That one had slipped right by them.

The back door opened and Hank stepped out. He was looking at some papers in his hand and didn't see Luke. It gave Luke time to study him. He was a tall man with broad shoulders just like Luke. That was a chilling realization. But there the resemblance ended. Hank's face was hard and he never smiled. If he did, Luke was sure his face would crack. On the other hand, Luke joked and laughed all the time.

Hank glanced up. "Luke."

Luke wasn't sure what to call him so he just nodded.

Hank gave him the once-over, from his slicked-down hair and a growth of beard that covered his scratches to his damp clothes and wet boots.

Hank stuffed the papers into his shirt pocket. "What happened to you?"

"Life happened. You happened."

"About that…"

Luke walked around him and went into the house. Lucy was in the kitchen with Clover. As she reached to put a cup in the cabinet, she spotted him. "Luke," she shouted, and the cup tumbled to the floor and broke into several pieces. She didn't even pause as she flew into his arms, wrapping hers tightly around his waist. "Oh, my baby. Are you okay?"

"Yes, Mom." His arms engulfed her. He

knew exactly what to call her. She would always be his mother.

Henry lumbered from the den. "Son, we need to talk."

He wanted to say "I'm not your son," but he didn't. He didn't want to hurt either one of them. He loved them. He was happy to realize that nothing about that had changed.

"First, I want to get cleaned up, and then I want answers."

"Yes. Yes." Lucy stroked his hair. "Go ahead. We'll be waiting."

Luke walked toward the stairs feeling old, feeling spent. He didn't even think as he showered and shaved. He'd done enough of that.

Fifteen minutes later, he was back in the kitchen. Henry, Lucy and Hank sat at the table drinking coffee. When Clover saw him, she hurried to him and grabbed his face, pulling him toward her and planting a big kiss on his forehead. Without a word, she went to her room.

Luke straddled a chair and Lucy noticed the scratches. "Oh, my goodness…"

"I'm okay, Mom." He scooted forward, his eyes on Hank. "Who is my mother?"

Henry and Lucy glanced at Hank.

"Jenna Crowder," Hank replied.

"Where is she?"

"She died giving birth."

He felt a moment of sadness. He'd thought that Henry and Lucy had bought him from his mother like a calf at auction—to the highest bidder.

He moved uncomfortably, hating that cynicism in him. "What happened?"

Henry and Lucy once again glanced at Hank.

"Jenna's father was dead, and she and her mother, Doris, moved from the panhandle to River Bluff to live with her mother's sister. Jenna had blond hair and blue eyes and I was crazy about her. She was fifteen and I was sixteen and we thought we were grown. But we were just kids playing grown-up games."

Hank stared into his coffee cup. "When she discovered she was pregnant, we just ignored it in hopes that it would go away." Hank paused. "Her mother noticed she was putting on weight and suspected the cause. Jenna told her and they decided Jenna would keep the baby and her mother would help raise it. Jenna was happy and I was relieved."

"Fits your character," Luke said, unable to stop the words.

Hank's eyes narrowed. "I was sixteen, Luke. I didn't want a kid. I was a kid myself."

Luke held his tongue.

"You were due in October so Jenna finished out the school year in May and then she and her mother moved to San Antonio. I didn't see her after that. Doris's sister called one day to say Jenna had died." Luke noticed Hank's knuckles were white as he gripped his cup. "Seems Jenna was spotting heavily and told no one. I guess she thought it would go away like the pregnancy. She passed out from the loss of blood and was rushed to the emergency room. They did an emergency C-section, but Jenna died on the table."

Luke's throat felt as raw as his emotions and he wanted to stop. He didn't want to hear any more, but he'd never been a coward so he waited for the rest of the story.

"I didn't know what to do. I figured Doris would take the baby, but the sister called a couple of days later and said Doris was taking Jenna's death hard. They had to sedate her. The next day she called again to say Doris wanted nothing to do with the baby and a doctor was admitting her to a mental institution until she could cope with her daughter's death." Hank took a breath. "They were putting the baby up for adoption."

Luke kept waiting.

"The baby would go to strangers and I couldn't let that happen so I told Mom and Pa. After getting the biggest lecture of my life…"

"You deserved every bit of it," Henry snapped.

Lucy placed her hand on Henry's arm to stop him.

Hank continued. "We went to San Antonio to see you."

"Oh." Lucy held a hand to her chest. "You were the most beautiful sight and the moment we saw those eyes, that hair and precious face, we knew you were ours."

Henry scowled. "It's all right for you to talk, but I can't."

"Sorry," Lucy said. "That just slipped out."

Hank again took up the story. "After we saw you, Mom and Pa talked to CPS and the adoption was set in motion. Pa hired an attorney and they brought you home within the week. But Pa laid down conditions, as always. I was to stay out of your life. We would be raised as brothers until you were older and ready to hear the truth."

"But you never told me."

"I was going to tell you after high school, but then you crashed the Mustang and joined the army. And I didn't want to tell you when you were on leave. I was afraid you'd get yourself killed."

"I've been home over six months. Why haven't you told me before now? And when you didn't have to drown yourself in liquor to do it."

"He wasn't ever going to do it until I forced the issue."

Everyone looked at Henry.

"The near-drowning made me think. Life is too unpredictable. We never know when our time is up and Luke deserved to know the truth, so I had to give Hank a little push. The only thing that would get his attention was dividing the land, something unheard of in the Chisum family. The ranch always goes to the firstborn son."

"You lied." Hank's lips curled back like an angry dog's.

"Yep, but I didn't break my word. Henry Chisum never breaks his word. You'll give this land to Luke just like you're supposed to."

Luke had reached his limit. He rose, feeling the hurt and anger bubbling in himself. "Is this some kind of game to the both of you? This is my life you're talking about and instead of being worried about my shattered life, you're more concerned that some Chisum tradition is upheld. Well, you can have the damn land. I don't want it." He swung toward the door.

"Luke," his mother called.

He whirled back. "It would have been nice if one of you had the gumption to say 'I'm sorry, Luke, for screwing up your life.' And it would have been refreshing if one of you had asked for my forgiveness."

"Chisums don't forgive, boy," Henry said. "We just accept."

"Well, accept this." He slammed the door so hard it shook the frame. He jumped into his truck and headed for River Bluff.

And Becky.

As HE REACHED TOWN, Luke realized it was after lunch so he stopped at the Longhorn for a bite. Everyone stared at him, but didn't say anything.

Thanks, Knut.

He knew his paternity was all over town thanks to Harold and the beauty-shop gossips. Luke ordered chicken-fried steak and Stefi, the waitress, didn't come on to him the way she usually did.

They'd gone to high school together and the boys had dubbed her Amazon Barbie. She was tall, gorgeous and popular. But after a couple of failed marriages, she was back in River Bluff waiting tables. It seemed Bobbie Sue was right—River Bluff was like a magnet drawing them all back.

Stefi set a glass of tea in front of him. He sipped on it as he waited, trying to avoid all the stares.

As Stefi placed the steak in front of him, she asked, "Are you doing okay, Luke?"

"Yeah. Why wouldn't I be?"

"No reason."

Ed hurried from the back. "Luke, I didn't know you were here." His New Jersey accent always sounded odd among all the Texas drawls. Ed glanced at Stefi, who was still lingering. "That table in the corner needs cleaning."

She made a face at Ed behind his back and walked away.

"Sometimes she's a little too friendly and nosy," Ed whispered. "Do you need anything?"

God, he hated how they were treating him with kid gloves. He wanted to tell them to stop the damn nervous treatment.

Instead, he held up his tea glass. "A refill would be nice."

"Sure. You got it."

Luke left the café as soon as he could and realized it was early. Becky was still at school. He drove to the Wild Card. Jake's truck wasn't there and workers were busy inside, so he walked through the pecan grove to the water's edge. The Wild Card was taking shape. The font porch was completely rebuilt and not in danger of collapsing. Soon Jake would be able to open the doors to the public. But not before the Not So Wild Bunch celebrated in style.

He picked up a rock and sailed it across the water. It fell flat after one skip. He didn't have the spirit to skip rocks today. He sank down onto the grass and rested his arms on his knees.

The sun bore down on him but the breeze

was cool as the scent of the old gray cypresses wafted to him. Memories of his childhood. So many times he and Jake had sailed rocks off the surface of the water, grumbling about their rotten lives.

In truth though, Jake had dealt with a lot more than Luke ever had. Until now… Luke was fighting to stay above the surface. He clasped his hands. He shouldn't have gotten so angry at Henry and Hank. But an "I'm sorry" would have healed a lot of wounds.

Chisums don't forgive. They accept.

Bullshit.

Jake eased down by him and slapped him on the back. "Hey, Luke."

Luke glanced at his friend. "Jake."

They sat in silence, not needing to talk. They knew each other well enough to know when talking wouldn't help.

"Want to skip some rocks?" Jake asked.

"No. I'm not in the mood."

"How about a beer?"

"No, thanks. I've had enough liquor to last for the next year."

They didn't say anything else.

"Becky and I reconnected," Luke finally said.

Jake slapped him on the back again.

"That's really good news. I'm glad something's going your way."

"The thought of her is keeping me sane."

"Luke…"

"I'm not going to do anything stupid." He rose to his feet. "I was just killing time until school lets out so I can see Becky." He walked toward his truck.

"Luke."

He turned back.

"I'm sorry, man."

Luke nodded. And to keep everything on a manly and not-too-sensitive track, he added, "The Card's coming along." His gaze slid beyond the pecan grove to the new house under construction. "And so is the house."

Jake grinned. "Never thought I'd see the day I would even think about living in River Bluff."

Again, to keep things on a manly keel, Luke picked up a rock and sailed it across the water. It skipped six times before it dropped below the surface. "Hot damn. I still got it."

"Was there ever any doubt?"

"Hell, no."

Jake gave a thumbs-up sign.

Luke walked to his truck with a swing in his step.

BECKY'S CAR WASN'T at the school so he drove to the clinic. Her car wasn't there, either, and the nurse said she wasn't scheduled to work again until Monday. This was Friday. Where was she?

CHAPTER FIFTEEN

BECKY PACED IN ANNIE'S living room. "I'm so worried about Luke."

Annie patted the spot beside her on the sofa. "Sit down, please, and have some tea."

Becky did as her friend suggested. After a few sips of Annie's special tea, she felt better. Placing her cup in the saucer, she said, "I shouldn't even be bothering you."

Annie frowned. "What do you mean you shouldn't be bothering me? We've been friends forever and we can talk about anything—even when I'm pregnant."

"I just don't want you to worry about me."

Annie took a sip of her tea. "Friends worry about friends."

Becky fingered her cup. "I just don't know how to tell him."

"You'll find the right words because you know you have to do it."

"Yes," she replied in a melancholy tone

and touched Annie's stomach. Luke had missed so much of Shane's life and she wondered if there would ever be a right time or the right words. She pushed those thoughts aside as she looked at her friend. "The baby's really growing."

"Yes, he or she is." Annie glowed with pleasure as she rubbed her stomach.

"You're sticking to your decision not to know the sex until it's born?"

"Yes, and Blake agrees with me."

"If you wanted to dye your hair purple, Blake would agree with you."

Annie smiled. "Love is wonderful."

Becky sighed.

"What is it?" Annie asked, noticing her expression.

"I love Luke. I guess I'm always going to love him and right now things are good between us. But when I tell him the truth, he's going to hate me."

Annie reached for Becky's hand. "Honesty is the only thing that's going to make the relationship work this time."

"Luke has been through so much."

"If you keep looking, you can find all kinds of excuses."

Becky grimaced. "I hate it when you make me face reality."

"It's not going to be easy, but raising Shane alone hasn't been easy, either." She patted Becky's hand. "You can do this."

Becky swallowed. "I guess I just needed to hear you say that."

The door opened and Blake walked in. Becky got to her feet and kissed his cheek. "I've got to run. Shane is having friends over for a campout and I have to pick them up."

"Girls or boys?" Annie asked as she kissed her husband.

Becky rolled her eyes. "Very funny. I'll see you two later."

"Bec," Blake called.

With a hand on the doorknob, she glanced at him.

"I saw Jake and he said Luke was in town earlier."

"He's back?"

"That's what Jake said."

"How is Luke?"

"A little down but okay."

So many questions zipped through her mind. The number-one question was why hadn't he called her?

"Did Jake say anything else?"

"No. We're just glad Luke is back and coping."

Becky shook her head. "Why can't guys ask questions?"

Annie lifted an eyebrow. "Don't go there. It's one of those things that can't be explained."

Blake looked from one to the other. "What?"

Annie wrapped her arms around him. "It's okay, honey. I love you anyway."

"I've got to run," Becky said.

"Call me," Annie shouted after her.

Becky crawled into her car and headed for the school to pick up Shane and his friends. She wanted to go to Great Oaks, but Luke would call when he was ready to talk. She wondered how things were going with his parents and Hank. That he was back was the main thing.

Now they could sort out the future.

LUKE WENT INTO San Antonio to buy new boots. He'd ruined his best pair and he didn't like the ones he was wearing. The new ones fit like a glove. Now if he could just keep them dry.

He drove to Great Oaks. Becky should be

home by now and he'd call her later when they would have time to be together. He was sure she was busy with her son at this hour.

When he walked into the breakfast room, his mom was sitting at the table paying bills. Her glasses were perched on the end of her nose. She usually paid bills in the study. What was she doing at the kitchen table? Then it dawned on him—she was waiting for him to come home.

He noticed Henry was in the den watching a sports channel.

Lucy looked up. "I'm glad you're back, son."

He plopped into a chair. "Where's Hank?"

Lucy removed her glasses and laid them on the table. "He's gone to tell Marla about you."

Oh God, he hadn't even thought about Marla. And Chelsea.

He cleared his throat. "I have a sister."

"Yes. You do." She folded the checkbook and bills, and laid them aside. "I want you to listen to me."

"Okay." He rubbed a spot on the table.

"I'm sorry you were hurt. I'm sorry Hank told you like that. But most of all I'm sorry

I let this go on so long. You should have been told years ago."

He looked up. "Why didn't you?"

Lucy shrugged. "I'm not sure. Henry left it up to Hank and the time was never right. You were a happy, mischievous kid and we didn't want to hurt you."

"That didn't exactly work out, did it?"

"No. Secrets always cause pain, but I'll never regret adopting you. You've been the joy of our lives."

"And the sorrow?"

"Yes. Crashing the Mustang and joining the army just about did us in. But that was nothing compared to the call we got when your helicopter went down. We couldn't travel because of Henry's stroke, but neither one of us slept until Hank called and had seen you at Walter Reed and said you were okay."

Hank was the first person Luke had seen when he'd woken up in the government hospital. Hank had stayed for two weeks until Luke had insisted he go home to help their parents because they needed him more.

Hank had been there.

Luke had forgotten that.

Another memory surfaced. Hank had been

the first person at the hospital when Luke had sailed the Mustang into the Medina River. He'd never left. Funny, he'd forgotten that, too.

Other memories intruded—more painful ones.

Luke leaned forward and rested his forearms on the table. "When I was growing up, Hank was on my ass all the time. Why was he so hard on me?"

"That was Henry's and my fault. We spoiled you, and Hank wanted you to grow up responsible and learn how to work for things instead of always having them given to you. That's why he wanted you to learn to run the ranch. It will one day be yours whether you want it or not. He couldn't tell you that he was your father, but he wanted your life to be better than his." Lucy fiddled with her glasses. "He didn't want you getting a girl pregnant in high school and living with the guilt, as he has all these years."

"Well, Mom, Hank really needs to work on his social skills."

Lucy laughed, a tinkling sound that floated through the room. "Luke, you always make me laugh."

"I never felt Hank cared about me one way or the other. I was just an annoyance to him."

"He does care, Luke. He just doesn't know how to show it."

"If you say so." But Luke wasn't so sure. He and Hank had a long way to go and he didn't know if the years could be bridged even with an "I'm sorry."

His mother's eyes clouded with worry, and he got up and hugged her. "I guess we can get through this."

She touched his face. "Yes, we can. We're Chisums."

"What's so funny?" Henry asked, walking into the room with his cane. Neither of them had heard him get up. "Lu was laughing."

"We're just talking, Henry," Lucy replied.

Henry looked at Luke. "You over your mad spell?"

"Maybe. Maybe not."

"Sit down," Henry ordered.

"I'm not really in a mood to go over this again."

"Sit down."

Luke clenched his jaw and complied.

Henry eased into a chair. "Now listen and

listen good because I'm only going to say this once." He took a breath. "I'm sorry." He swallowed as if the words tasted bitter. "But if I had the opportunity to go back, I wouldn't change a thing. You've brightened our lives. Scared the hell out of us more than once and gave us memories we'll never forget. You're a Chisum, through and through, and it's time to accept that. It's time to put your foot in the stirrup and grab the reins."

Luke didn't laugh because his dad was so serious. This was Henry, hardnosed and driven to a fault. This was the father Hank dealt with every day of his life. This was Luke's first taste of the stern, unyielding Henry.

Through that realization, one thing stood out. This was as close to an apology as he was going to get. And Luke found it was enough.

"Thanks, Pa."

Henry eyed him. "You hugged your mother. Why aren't you hugging me?"

Because you're an ass.

But he stood and hugged the only father he'd ever known. Henry's hands shook as they gripped Luke, and Luke felt tears sting his eyes. Love was a powerful thing. It made forgiving easy.

Even for a Chisum.

LUKE WENT UP to his room and called Becky. Shane was going camping with some friends and she was busy getting him off. Luke planned to go over later.

He sat on the bed for a moment and pondered how things had changed so much in a few days. His whole life had changed. He and Becky had gotten beyond the past and that made him strong enough to handle whatever life threw at him.

They would talk about the future and their lives. This time they would take it slow and make the right decisions. They weren't eager teenagers anymore.

But a part of him was always going to be an eager teenager in love with Becky. Now they had to fall in love as adults. Luke felt he was already there and he knew Becky was, too. But she had a son, and he knew she had to think about Shane and his future. She wouldn't do anything to upset Shane. Luke didn't want her to, either.

They had to take the kid's feelings into consideration. Shane had a father, and Luke had no desire to replace Danny. And he didn't know anything about kids, but he liked Shane even though he was a little headstrong.

Ramming his hands through his hair, he rose to his feet. He had to sort through the tangled mess of his own paternity. He wondered how Marla was taking the news of a thirty-four-year-old stepson. With her usual tact, he was sure. But she was probably going to be angry that Hank had kept his son a secret all these years.

Luke was still angry himself.

Forgiveness for Hank would not come so easily.

WHEN HE DROVE into the Parkers' yard, Luke saw Becky sitting on the front steps, the porch light reflecting off her auburn hair. He got out, opened the gate in the chain-link fence and strolled up the walk. In his teens, he'd done this so many times it now brought back vivid memories. One in particular was Hub knocking him into the yard with a right jab that still had Luke reeling. Mostly, it brought back memories of Becky—the taste and feel of her.

Easing his frame down beside her, he

slipped his arm around her and pulled her to him. His lips took hers in a long, deep kiss. He tasted her, savored the feeling that erased all his pain. After a moment, he trailed a path from her lips to her cheek to her ear and then to her neck.

"I've been wanting to do that all day," he whispered, breathing in her fresh lemony scent.

She stroked his face, and he turned his head and planted a kiss in her palm.

"How are you?" she asked, examining his healing scratches in the moonlight. Her fingers felt like velvet against his skin.

"I feel as if I've been put through a meat grinder."

"I'm sorry." She hugged him. "How did the talk go with your parents and Hank?"

He told her everything he'd learned.

"So your mother is dead?"

"Yes. My parents did the only thing they could—they adopted me so I would be raised as a Chisum."

Becky drew back, feeling guilty and afraid. "But Hank is the reason they adopted you."

"Yeah, after he'd screwed up his courage to tell them he got a girl pregnant in high school." He kissed her forehead. "I'd rather not talk about Hank."

"You have to," she told him. "To go forward, you have to forgive him."

He stilled. "I don't think I can do that, Bec. All these years he knew I was his son and he treated me like dirt."

"I'm sure keeping that kind of secret was hard on Hank."

"Are we talking about the same Hank?" His voice grew angry. "The same Hank who berated me for being lazy, irresponsible and spoiled. The same Hank who said I'd amount to nothing and that I didn't have what it took to make it in the United States Army."

"Luke." She wrapped her arms around him.

He buried his face in her neck. "Don't ask me to forgive him. I can't."

"He is your father."

"Biologically only."

"I know you're not a hard person and eventually you'll see that everyone makes mistakes."

"I don't know, Becky. Pa said Chisums never forgive. They just accept. That made me angry at the time, but now I believe it's true. I'll never forgive Hank, but for my parents I'll accept him."

Her heart stopped beating and she felt the pain of it in her chest. Luke wasn't ever going to forgive her, either. The coward in her reared its ugly head and she wanted to keep her secret forever. To grab at the new love they'd found. But she couldn't have a relationship with Luke built on a lie.

She had to tell him. It might help him to see that everyone made mistakes—even him and her. But in her heart, she knew once she said the words *Shane is your son,* their relationship would be over for good. Luke and Shane would forge a bond and hopefully, through the heartache and pain, Luke could look at Hank a little differently. Maybe somewhere in the pain she was about to heap on him, he could find a measure of forgiveness for his father.

But for her, it would be different. Luke would see her as someone he couldn't trust. As someone he couldn't love. The hard truth was that secrets destroyed lives. By taking the easy way out years ago, she would now have to face the consequences, the pain and the disillusionment.

He planted a kiss in the curve of her neck,

making her senses spin and her resolve waver.

"Where is everyone?" he asked in a hoarse voice.

"Dad's asleep in his chair and Shane's camped out on Cypress Creek with his friends."

"Oh. I was hoping we were alone." She heard his disappointment.

"We are, in a way. We have the sky for an umbrella."

"Mmm." He drew back, viewing the magical display. "So the kid's roughing it?"

She noticed he always called Shane *the kid*. "That's what he calls it, but you should see the stuff they took."

"I bet there was a cooler of beer."

"Brad brought a cooler and I really wanted to look inside, but they're out in the woods, so I just have to trust my son." She brushed back her hair. "It's not easy letting fifteen-year-old boys be fifteen-year-old boys, especially when you're a mother."

She tried to keep the fear out of her voice and failed.

"Doesn't Danny help with him?"

"Not a lot. I've raised Shane by myself."

She looked off to the darkened sky, trying to find the words. "Danny has tried, but it's hard juggling his attention between his kids and Shane."

He pulled her to him again and she didn't resist. Her body was starved for his touch. They sat listening to the night sounds and watching the breathtaking panoramic view of the sky.

Rubbing her face against his, she knew once again the moment wasn't right. Shane was too close, and she wanted him out of the way when she told Luke. Her first instinct was always to protect her son.

"When can we be alone?" he asked, his hand stroking her arm.

"Danny's picking up Shane about eleven in the morning and he's spending the day in San Antonio with Danny and his family."

"So we have tomorrow afternoon?"

"Yes. My dad has his domino game on Saturday afternoons with his old law-enforcement buddies."

"Just you and me then."

"Just you and me," she echoed, resting her head on his shoulder and allowing herself this moment of being young and so in love that nothing else mattered.

Tomorrow that would change.

Tomorrow would bring reality.

CHAPTER SIXTEEN

THE NEXT MORNING nothing went right. Shane and his friends wanted to spend another night in the woods camping, so Shane wanted her to call Danny and tell him he'd come another time. Becky refused to do it.

Shane was in a bad mood after that, but he was clean and ready to go when Danny drove up.

He hugged Shane and said they had to hurry because they were meeting Noreen and the kids for lunch, then they were going to look at trucks. Shane immediately perked up.

As they got ready to leave, Shane paused. "Wait. I left my watch in the four wheeler. I'll be right back." He flew out the door.

"You seem nervous," Danny remarked.

"I'm telling Luke this afternoon." Danny had a right to know.

He nodded. "That's good. Do you need me to do anything?"

"No, Danny. You've done enough."

He looked at her. "I wish you could have loved me the way you loved him."

She met his eyes. "I'm sorry I dragged you into this."

"I went willingly, Becky. You didn't have to twist my arm, and to be honest, I'm grateful. It opened my eyes. You can't make someone love you. It's either there or it isn't. It was never there for us, but I have that with Noreen."

"I'm so glad you found happiness."

He shoved his hands into his pockets. "Thank you. I hope you and Luke can work this out. You deserve to be happy."

"I lied to him, Danny. I don't see any happiness in my future."

"Then Luke is a fool. He's not blameless in this."

She touched her hand to the throb in her forehead. "Danny, please."

There was silence for a moment.

"Do you want me to be here when you tell Shane?"

"No, thank you. I have to do this alone. He's my son."

"Becky…"

"Are you ready, Dad?" Shane burst through the door.

"Yes. Let's hit the road." He glanced at Becky. "Bye."

"Bye," she responded and hugged her son. "I love you."

"Ah, Mom. You don't have to tell me that all the time."

She did, especially today.

"Have a good time," she called as they walked out the door.

"We're going to eat at that Tex-Mex place you like," Danny was telling Shane.

"Awesome," was Shane's response. "I'm ordering the double-decker enchilada plate with nachos and maybe guacamole."

Becky was always staggered by her son's appetite, but she knew someone who could match it.

Luke.

She closed the door, bracing herself for the rest of this day.

LUKE HAD BREAKFAST with his parents and Hap. Hank wasn't back, so Luke assumed he was still at Marla's explaining his ass off. Luke was sure an apology wasn't forthcoming. That wasn't Hank's style. Luke planned to visit Marla and Chelsea later in the week.

He spent the morning at the barn checking in maize that would last for another week. Hap had it under control, but Luke had to stay busy. Most of the cowboys were off today, so there was a restful calm about the place.

He fed the paints and headed back to the house. His cell buzzed. It was Jake.

"Hey, Luke. Want to flex your muscles?"

"Depends on where and what."

"The Wild Card. Cole and I are putting up the last beam and we could use some extra muscle. I'm trying to reach Brady, too."

"Normally I'd say yes, but I have a date with Becky this afternoon."

"Hot damn. You're not wasting any time."

"Nope."

"We're not going to do this until about five and then we're meeting the girls for dinner. Maybe you and Becky can join us."

"I'll see what she says."

"Man, this is like old times."

"And we're a hell of a lot older."

Luke heard Jake laugh as he clicked off. He hurried to shower and change, counting the minutes until he could be with Becky.

BECKY'S DAY only got worse. Her father refused to leave.

"I'm not leaving you alone with him," Hub said stubbornly.

"Dad, you can't fix this for me. I have to do it and I have to do it alone."

"He'll be angry."

"I'm aware of that."

"He might hurt you."

Becky sighed. "Luke is not going to hurt me. I'm going to hurt him in a way he doesn't deserve. That's my fault and I have to take full responsibility, so please go to your domino game. I'll be fine."

Begrudgingly, her dad left and she took a seat on the step to wait. She thought of putting on something nice, but they weren't going anywhere, so there was no need to dress up or to pretend.

She saw the cloud of dust a moment before she saw his truck. Her breath caught as he got out and strolled up the walk in his loose-limbed way. He was six foot two inches tall and at a petite five foot four inches, she often felt dwarfed by his height and breadth of shoulder. He was tall, strong and unbelievably attractive. That was why at an insecure seventeen she couldn't believe he'd really loved her. That doubt had cost her so much.

He was older now, but still devastatingly handsome. The sharp lines of his face were more defined, and that raw-boned vitality and five o'clock shadow still turned her knees to putty. If she squinted, she could see the young boy who'd swaggered up her walk with more confidence than Evel Knievel. If she squinted even more, she could see Shane, and she wondered why Luke had never thought Shane might be his.

"Hi, Bec." He sat beside her and kissed her briefly, smiling into her eyes. "I have this fantasy. Want to know what it is?"

"Yes." His humor was always infectious.

"You and I making love in a bed." His dark eyes stared into hers. "Think we can make that happen?"

Once again her resolve weakened, and she wanted to forget everything and live in the moment. But the adult Becky shouldered a responsibility she couldn't ignore.

"I'd like to talk first."

He rested his forearms on his knees. "Sure."

"When you were gone all those years, did you ever think about me?"

He looked at her. "Are you asking if I've been with other women?"

"No." She shook her head. "I'm asking if you thought about me."

"Sure, all the time." He rubbed his large hands together. "I kept seeing you and Danny kissing at the gas station. And I remembered how much it hurt that you didn't come to the hospital after they rescued me from the Medina River."

She licked her dry lips. "I was there."

"What?" Those dark eyes widened.

"I slipped into ICU and sat by your side until about six in the morning. You never woke up, but you were breathing and I knew you were alive. I met Lucy when I was leaving."

"She never said anything."

"With all the tension afterward, I guess she forgot."

"Yeah. Hank pretty much went berserk, trying to finish me off with his ranting and raving about what an idiot I was."

"I think he was just afraid of how close he came to losing you."

His eyes narrowed. "You're joking, right?"

"No. I think Hank cares for you, but he

was so young when you were born that he didn't know how to show it."

"Are you taking up for him?"

"No. I'm trying to get you to see there are reasons why people do what they do."

"I'll never understand how he could treat his own son like he did—to pretend that I didn't exist. I could never do that to a son of mine."

She swallowed hard. "But you did."

"What!"

She gripped her hands until they were numb. "That time you saw Danny and me at the gas station, we weren't kissing."

"It sure looked like it."

"I was upset and he was trying to comfort me."

He frowned. "What the hell does it matter? We can't go back and change the past."

Becky took a long breath, trying to get through this. "I was upset because I'd just discovered I was pregnant."

She waited, but he didn't say anything. He just kept staring at her with a dark, foreboding expression.

As hard as it was, she forced the next words out. "Danny said I had to tell you, but

I was in shock and I didn't know what to do. I was afraid of my father, the gossip. But after I thought about it, I knew I had to. I couldn't handle it alone so I went to Great Oaks, and Lucy was crying and Henry wouldn't talk. Hank said you'd joined the army. You once told me that if you ever left River Bluff, you were never coming back." She paused for a breath.

Luke kept staring at her as if he were in a trance.

"I had to face reality and do what was best for my child. Danny asked me to marry him and I was happy to have someone to lean on. We told my dad and we were married quickly and moved to San Antonio."

Slowly, Luke rose to his feet. "Shane is *my* son?" His face was ashen, his voice rough.

"Yes."

"And you've kept it from me all these years?"

"You weren't here to tell."

"My mother knew where I was at all times. All you had to do was ask."

"I wasn't thinking too clearly. I made wrong choices for the right reasons."

"Like hell!" he shouted. "There's nothing

right about this. You kept my son from me. How could you do that? The one person in the world who I thought I could trust has betrayed me in a way no man should ever have to live with!"

"I'm sorry." She gulped back tears.

"*Sorry* doesn't even begin to cut it."

"Luke." She stood on wobbly legs. "You never thought once that Shane could be yours?"

"Hell no!"

"Why not?"

"Don't turn this around on me, Becky." He swiped a hand through his hair. "Does Shane know?"

She shook her head. "I haven't told him."

He pointed a finger at her. "I want it done as soon as possible. Do you hear me?"

She nodded, tears blocking her throat.

"All these years I've been waiting for you to forgive me. Forgive me? That's a laugh, isn't it?"

"Luke…"

"And the concern and the sex by the pond were just to soften me up for this… this truth session?"

"No. My feelings for you have never changed."

"That's a little late."

"Luke," she cried.

"You just destroyed everything I've ever felt for you and I'll never forgive you. Never!"

She bit down on her lip to keep from crying out, but it wouldn't have done any good. Luke wouldn't have heard her or cared. All he could feel was his own pain.

A pain she'd inflicted.

LUKE JUMPED INTO his truck and drove away. He wanted to burn rubber, spin his tires, do something dangerous. Reckless. But he drove steadily toward River Bluff.

The woman he'd loved most of his life had deceived him.

I have a son.

A son she'd kept from him.

Was he supposed to just accept that? He could feel the anger and pain churning inside him like sour milk. He felt sick, and the bile rose up in his throat. All his hopes and dreams had ended in a split second.

Shane is my son.

He looked up and saw he was at the Wild Card. Jake, Cole, Brady and Blake's vehicles were there. Why was he here? He'd forgotten.

He suddenly saw Becky's face and the tears streaming down it. But he wouldn't let her get to him. Not ever again. That helpless, sinking feeling crept over him. He was going down. He had to do something.

A tap on his window startled him. "Luke, why aren't you getting out?" Cole asked.

When Luke didn't respond, Cole opened the door. "C'mon, Luke. We're about ready to hoist the beam and then we're rewarding ourselves with beer."

Somehow Luke found himself out of the truck. He followed Cole to the front porch that faced the Medina River, but the feeling stopped him dead. He had to run. He had to get away.

Brady, Jake and Blake stood on the porch staring at him. He was vaguely aware of them coming toward him.

"Luke, what's wrong?" Cole asked.

He heard Cole's voice and it came from far away.

"Luke." Jake's and Brady's voices blended together. He felt Blake's arm as it went around his shoulder.

He fought the feeling and tried to focus on his friends.

"What is it, Luke?" Brady asked. "What

happened? Did you have a fight with Hank?"

"I have a son," he managed to say through parched lips.

"Wh-at?" Jake leaned closer. "I didn't catch that."

"Shane is my son."

Complete silence followed those words.

"Who told you that?" Cole wanted to know

"Becky," he replied. "She kept it a secret all these years. How could she do that? How could she hurt me like this?" The feeling engulfed him. "I have to get away. I can't handle this."

Run. Run. Run. That was all he could hear. He had to find shelter and safety.

He swung toward his truck, but Jake grabbed one arm; Brady had the other. Cole put a hammerlock on him from behind.

"Just calm down and listen." Blake tried to reason with him.

But he felt the fear and the need to run. But like the barbed wire, the arms held him in a snare.

"Let me go," he shouted, fighting to get away. He jerked and pulled. The arm around his neck tightened, but Luke fought that much harder. In the struggle, the four men tumbled to the ground. Luke kept fighting.

"Stop it," Jake shouted.

"Luke, goddammit, it's us." Brady's voice hissed in his ear.

Finally his energy was spent and he stilled.

"Luke?" Cole asked, his arm loosening around Luke's neck. "Are you okay?"

"No, dammit, you're about to choke me."

"Well, stop fighting," Jake told him.

"Okay, Luke," Brady said. "We're going to let go. Don't do anything stupid or I'll have to knock you out."

"In your dreams." Luke sat up, flexing his shoulders. "Damn, I didn't know you guys were that strong."

Jake stretched his arm. "You're like a raging bull."

They were quiet for a moment as they sat on the ground, trying to catch their breath.

Luke knew his friends had saved him from doing something stupid. They knew him well.

"Thanks, guys," he said.

"You okay, Luke?" Blake watched him closely.

"No. I'll never be the same again." He

drew up his knees. "Nothing will ever be the same again."

"But you have a son," Blake reminded him. "That's an incredible gift."

"Yeah." He stared down at the ground. "And it's ironic. Shane is going to dislike me as much as I dislike Hank."

There was silence again.

"Luke, this is Becky we're talking about." Cole spoke up. "Give her a chance to explain. I'm sure she did the best she could at the time."

"No." Luke pushed to his feet. "Becky doesn't get any more chances from me."

"What about Shane?" Jake asked.

Luke ran his hands over his face in total despair. "Man, I don't know. I feel as if someone has ripped out my guts and I'm struggling to just keep breathing."

"Let's go get a beer," Blake suggested.

"No. I'm going home and try to figure out why everyone close to me thinks I have rubber emotions. Everything bounces off ol' Luke. Let me tell you, this ain't bouncing. This sucks."

"I'm sorry, man, but you're strong. You'll bounce back."

"Take a good look at me, Brady. I'm

down and out. I've reached my quota of shocks. And I've reached my limit of being hurt by the people I love."

"That sucks," Cole said.

"I'm sorry, Luke," Jake added his thoughts.

"If you need anything, just call me." Blake patted his shoulder.

"Thanks, guys. And thanks for wrestling some sense into me."

"I'm sending you the cleaning bill for these jeans." Brady brushed dirt from his clothes.

"Send away." Luke turned toward his truck. "Send it in care of I don't give a rat's ass."

"Luke's back," Jake said.

He nodded. "Yeah. Now I'm going home and see what I can salvage of my pride and my life."

He drove away knowing there wasn't anything to salvage.

Becky had destroyed it all.

CHAPTER SEVENTEEN

BECKY CRIED UNTIL there were no tears left. She managed to pull herself together before her father arrived home, but then she burst into tears all over again. By the time Danny brought Shane back, she was in control, or as near as possible under the circumstances.

Shane was in his room looking through truck brochures and she stood in the kitchen watching the clock on the wall, the seconds ticking away.

"You're going to stare a hole in that clock," Hub said, finishing a glass of tea from supper.

She took a long breath. "I guess I'd better tell him."

"Rebecca, Shane is a good kid. He'll be angry, but he'll get over it."

"I just hate the thought of hurting him."

"You knew that one day you'd have to face this talk. It's here. You have to tell him before Luke does." He stood. "I'll be in the living room if you need me."

"Thanks, Dad."

She walked to her son's room. He lay on the bed in his jeans and sneakers, his head in a brochure.

"Hey, Mom," he said as he saw her, barely glancing up.

She sat down on the bed and scooted to face him.

"Mom." He placed a brochure in her lap. "Look at that truck. It's a monster and has tons of chrome. What do you think?"

The truck was a blur and she couldn't concentrate on it now. "Very nice," she replied. "Could we talk for a minute?"

"Sure." His eyes narrowed on her face. "Are you sick? You look pale."

That was always Shane's first question. One of his friends' mothers had died from cancer and she knew that worried Shane.

"I'm not sick," she reassured him.

"Are you sure? You kind of look like that time you had the flu."

"Shane, just listen to me."

"Okay, Mom. Don't have a cow."

She took several deep breaths. "I've done something very, very bad."

His eyes widened. "Are you gonna be arrested?"

She almost burst out laughing at the way a fifteen-year-old boy's mind worked. "No."

"Shoot, Mom, what could you do that was bad, anyway?"

She smoothed the fabric of her jeans. "In high school, Danny and I were the geeks. We excelled in our studies and stayed out of trouble. We weren't part of the jocks, cheerleaders and the popular crowds."

"So what?"

"Then someone dared one of the jocks to ask me out on a date. You see, they were all scared of the sheriff, your grandfather, and it was a macho thing to do. I didn't know about the dare and I was so excited when he asked me because I had a crush on him. We hit it off and we went out again. I was head-over-heels in love and I did something really stupid. I let my heart rule my emotions."

He made a face. "Jeez, Mom. I don't want to hear about your boyfriends in high school."

"Shane, please, just listen."

"Okay. Okay." He pushed up and sat cross-legged.

She sucked in a breath. "I loved him and I had sex with him."

"You had sex in high school?" She had his full attention.

"Yes." She forced herself to continue. "Then someone told me about the dare and I was crushed. I thought he cared about me, but all I could think was that he and his friends were laughing behind my back at how gullible I was. And I heard the kids talking and that made it worse. I wouldn't speak to him anymore or have anything else to do with him."

"I hope Grandpa kicked his ass."

"Shane."

"Oops. That slipped out."

"I turned to Danny then. We've always been very good friends." She tucked curls behind her ear, watching his face as she said the next words. "Soon I discovered I was pregnant and I didn't know what to do."

His expression changed completely. There was no laughter or teasing. Shane was quietly attentive to everything she was saying.

"I didn't have the best relationship with your grandfather at the time and I was scared to tell him. I was really frightened out of my mind, especially when the guy left town. I was all alone and I did the only thing I could at the time."

"You had an abortion? Was that the bad thing?"

"No. I married Danny."

His eyes narrowed in thought as he made the connection. "So Danny's not my real father?"

"No. And that's the bad thing. I should have told you before now."

"Why are you telling me now? I don't want to hear it." He placed his hands over his ears.

She reached up and pulled down his hands. "Because your real father is back and he wants to meet you."

"Who told him about me?"

"I did. He has a right to know."

"No, he doesn't," Shane shouted. "If I see him, I'll punch his lights out."

She slid over and put her arm around him. "I'm the bad person here. He didn't know anything about you. I never told him."

He brushed away an errant tear. "I don't care. I don't have to see him."

"No, you don't. I'll leave that up to you." She was giving him a choice when he had none, but she knew her son. Pressuring him would only make it worse.

"Good." He folded a brochure and placed

it on top of another one. "Who is he? Do I know him?"

"Yes. You know him."

"Who?" He looked straight at her.

She swallowed. "Luke Chisum."

"What!" His mouth fell open and she saw the anger she'd expected earlier blazing like a fire in his blue eyes. "I'm a Chisum?"

"Yes."

"All the times I've been on their property and they made me leave, saying I'm trespassing." His anger mounted and he swung off the bed. "I'm gonna kick his ass."

"Shane." But she was too late. He flew out the door. She was a step behind him, but in her haste she tripped and fell. By the time she scrambled to her feet and reached the back door, she saw Shane spinning out with the four wheeler, heading toward the Chisum property.

"What happened?" Hub asked, standing beside her.

"He's going to confront Luke. I couldn't stop him."

"But he's not going toward Great Oaks," Hub said, watching the cloud of dust. "He's headed south. Isn't that where the Chisums have the deer leases?"

"I have to call Luke." She sprinted for the house, worried about her son, worried what he might do.

Luke, please have your cell.

Please. Please.

LUKE DROVE DOWN the lane under the canopy of live oaks, trying to figure out what he had to do for his own peace of mind. His cell buzzed and he looked at the caller ID.

Becky.

How much more could he take today? He clicked on, needing to find out.

"Luke."

"What is it?"

"I told Shane and he said he was going to confront you, but he headed south on the four wheeler. I don't know where he's going and I'm worried."

"I'll find him." A sliver of alarm slid up his spine. The kid wasn't that stupid, was he?

"Luke."

That note in her voice was about to kill him.

"I'll call you later." He clicked off, not wanting to weaken in any way.

The south pasture was a good drive away and it was impossible to make it by truck. There was no way to cross Cypress Creek except to go through it on horseback or walk across in low places. He slammed on the brakes at the corral of the paints. The kid had a head start and Luke needed a fast horse.

The fastest one was Cochise, so Luke threw a saddle over his back. As he shot out of the barn, Luke didn't even want to think what Shane had in mind. He just had to reach him before he did anything stupid.

He rode Cochise hard and the paint was up to the task. Through fields, pastures, rocks and stones, the horse never faltered. Cypress Creek wasn't a problem, either. The horse swam across with ease. After that, Luke let him run because time was of the essence. It seemed like forever, but Luke knew they were covering ground quickly.

When they reached a thicket, Luke slowed, and Cochise picked his way through to a clearing. Luke saw the cabin and stopped, listening. He heard it instantly, the hum and grinding of the four wheeler.

Riding toward the low cliffs, he saw Shane as he aimed the wheeler toward the ledge at full throttle. Luke's pulse pounded hard in his ears. He was too far away to reach the kid.

It crossed his mind that all he could do was sit here and watch *his* kid die. And then he thought, how would he tell Becky?

Just then, Shane turned the wheel and spun away from the edge. But Luke knew he wasn't through. Shane just didn't have the speed he wanted. The boy stopped a farther distance away and gunned the throttle, taking another run at the cliff. Luke knew this was his last chance.

He kneed Cochise and drove the horse at a breakneck speed to reach Shane. The horse's hooves hit the ground harder and harder, and each stretch brought Luke closer and closer to the back of the four wheeler. Just when he knew there was no time left, Luke leaped from the saddle and made a dive for Shane. He had him was all that registered. He and Shane tumbled to the left. Cochise veered to the right. The wheeler went over the cliff and sank into the Medina River.

I've got him. I've got Shane.

It took a moment to catch his breath, but he felt the boy beneath him, alive, breathing and all in one piece.

The sun was sinking in the west and a late-evening breeze stirred. It had never felt so damn good. Luke sucked air into his starved lungs and rolled to his feet.

Shane came up fighting. He flew at Luke in a rage, hitting him with his fists and shouting, "I hate you! I hate you! I hate you!"

Luke tried to ward off the blows, but the kid was strong and Luke realized in a few years the boy would be as big as him.

"I hate you. I hate you," Shane railed on, his fists making contact with Luke's chest, arms and face. "How could you do that to my mother? How could you do that to her?" The blows kept coming. "How could you do that to her? How could you do that to me?"

The last word was dragged out in such pain that Luke locked his arms around Shane and once again they sank to the ground.

"Calm down, kid."

"My name is Shane," he screeched and tried to break free, but Luke held him tightly.

"I didn't know about you, Shane. I didn't know you were my son."

The fight went out of Shane and he sagged limply in Luke's arms.

"I'm sorry."

Shane wiped at his eyes, leaving mud trails on his face. "Why did you take a dare to go out with my mom?"

"It was a guy thing. You should understand that. But I liked her and it turned into so much more. The first date was a dare, but after that I went out with her because I wanted to."

"Why didn't you tell her?"

"I honestly forgot about it. Another guy thing."

Shane inched away. "I don't like you and I don't want you to be my father."

"Well, Shane, that ship has already sailed."

"My mom is the sweetest, nicest person in the whole world. How could you just leave her?"

"She wouldn't accept my apology and she wouldn't talk to me. Then she started dating Danny and it broke my heart. I had to leave River Bluff."

"But what about me?"

There was the question that was tearing them both apart.

"Listen to me, Shane. I didn't know Becky was pregnant. I didn't know anything about you."

Shane rubbed at his eyes. "Why not? You had sex with her. Why wouldn't it cross your mind?"

The truth of that hit him once again like Hub's right fist. But he wasn't going down this time. "Stupid, I guess."

"Yeah, real stupid."

Luke rose to his feet. "C'mon, Shane. It's time to take you back to your mother."

Shane stood and brushed off his clothes. "I can get myself back." He looked around. "Where's my wheeler?"

Luke thumbed toward the river.

Shane ran to the edge of the cliff and stared down into the murky water. In the waning light, there wasn't much to see.

"Jeez, what am I gonna tell Grandpa?"

Luke rubbed his jaw. "Well, for one thing, he won't need a DNA test to prove your paternity."

The corners of Shane's mouth twitched. "Yeah. I guess I get my stupidity from you."

Luke couldn't dispute that. He pointed below to the shadowy rocks. "Your body could be there. What would I have told your mother—that you sailed off this cliff without any regard for your life or hers?"

Shane hung his head.

"When I woke up in the hospital from the Mustang crash, I was hurting in every bone in my body. But that was nothing compared to the pain I felt when I looked into my mother's eyes and saw the disillusionment and the heartache. So before you even think about something so crazy again, you'd better think about your mother. If you don't, I'm going to make your life a living hell. And I learned from the very best—Hank Chisum. Do you understand me?"

"Yes." The boy kicked at the dirt, then added in a stubborn teenage voice, "I really thought I would make it."

Luke sighed and wanted to shake him. He wondered if Hank had felt the same way about him. This payback bull was hell.

"Let's go."

"You can't tell me what to do. You're not my…"

Luke faced him. "It's getting dark and my body is bruised from head to toe, but let's get one thing straight right here, right now. I'm your father. If you want to hit me some more, you go right ahead. But it's not going to change a thing."

"I don't like you and I'm not calling you Dad."

"I'm not asking you to." He whistled and Cochise trotted forward. Putting his boot in the stirrup, Luke swung up and held out his hand to Shane.

"I can walk," Shane said in true Chisum style.

Luke gritted his teeth and continued to hold out his hand. A battle of wills ensued, a standoff between father and son. But Luke knew this game well. He'd played it many times with Hank. Finally Shane gave in to the stronger power and placed his hand in Luke's.

With Shane behind him, they started the long trek home. They rode for a while in silence. In the thicket, the blackness of the night surrounded them. Luke didn't have that helpless, going-down feeling, and he was hoping it was gone for good. He wasn't running anymore. Safety was here in River Bluff facing life.

Facing Becky and Shane.

And Hank.

"Did you love my mother?" Shane asked.

"Yes."

They continued on, Cochise picking his way over rocks.

"If you had known about me, would you have married my mother?"

"Yes."

That was all the boy seemed to want to hear. Luke felt Shane's head as it rested against him. This was a hell of a way to bond, but at least it seemed to be working.

As they reached Cypress Creek, Shane stirred. Cochise glided through the water without a problem.

"This horse is awesome," Shane said. "I want a paint."

"Really?"

"Yep. And from now on no one tells me to get off Chisum land."

"I thought you didn't like me and didn't want me for a father."

"I don't, but like you said, I can't change it and I'm not stupid."

"Well, the jury is still out on that one, kid."

"My name is Shane."

"So you keep telling me."

"I still want a paint," Shane murmured, his head resting against Luke once again.

They continued in silence. When Luke reached the fence line between the Parkers and the Chisums, he said, "We're almost there."

From the outside lights Luke could see

Becky and Hub pacing by Hub's shop. As they rode in, Becky ran to meet them. Shane slipped to the ground and Becky grabbed him, hugging him and kissing his face.

"I'm sorry, Mom," Luke heard him mutter.

"It's all right," Becky replied, her eyes catching Luke's.

He wanted to look away, but he couldn't. Tears stained her face and her hair was frizzed out from running her fingers through it, he was sure. He saw her pain, her heart-ache and her sadness, and it touched every part of him. Once again, he'd hurt her. But she'd hurt him, too. And that was the part he couldn't get past.

Was this going to be a repeat of their high school years?

Becky turned, and she and Shane walked toward the house.

Shane didn't look back.

Neither did Becky.

CHAPTER EIGHTEEN

"WHERE'S THE FOUR WHEELER?" Hub asked.

Luke hadn't even realized Hub was still standing there. He'd been too engrossed in Becky and Shane walking away from him. Was there something symbolic in that? He couldn't help but feel there was.

He shook off the feeling.

"In the Medina River," he replied.

Even in the moonlight, Luke could see Hub's face turn three shades of gray. "What!"

Cochise moved restlessly and Luke patted his neck to calm him. "Shane tried to jump from one cliff to the other of the river."

"What happened?"

"I had to do a little rodeoing with a very fast horse. I reached him just as he neared the ledge."

"Thank God." Hub shook his head. "That boy just never learns."

Cochise pranced around and Luke pulled tight on the reins. Cochise snorted, but settled down.

The chirp of crickets filled the silence.

Luke moved edgily in the saddle. "She should have told me, Hub."

"You weren't here, boy."

"My mom knew where I was."

"Maybe that wasn't so easy for Rebecca." Hub scratched his head. "Maybe if I hadn't been so strict, she would have turned to me. But if we're going to pass around the blame pie, boy, you'd better take the biggest piece."

Luke nodded, realizing that was true. He wasn't blameless.

"I'll help you get the wheeler out tomorrow," he said, knowing it was time to start taking responsibility for a kid who was as wild as Luke had ever been. "It'll be dangerous for boaters if we leave it. Between a boat and the copter, I think we can get it out of harm's way."

Hub scratched his head again. "You've grown up, Luke Chisum."

Luke inclined his head and turned Cochise toward home.

"Luke."

He glanced back.

"Thanks."

"You're welcome."

Alone through the darkness he rode. Going home. A place he'd always dreamed of leaving, but now he dreamed of staying forever. He had a kid. That made a man grow up faster than a helicopter going down in the dead of night.

Bone-weary, he unsaddled Cochise and fed him. By the time he reached the house, the lights were out. Everyone was in bed. He trudged to the backyard and fell to the ground, stretching out on the cool St. Augustine grass.

He was spent emotionally and physically. Even his soul was spent. Every part of him had been tested to the limit today. And he'd survived—without the nightmare. His friends had been there to get him over the top.

The grass tickled his neck and a raindrop fell on his forehead. Or he hoped it was a raindrop. He didn't have the strength to brush it away nor did he have the strength to move. Through the weblike oak branches, he glimpsed the brilliant sky and its many sparkling lights. Magical stars—that was what Becky used to call them. She flittered across his mind like those wisps of light, elusive and out of his reach.

The magic was gone.

His eyes closed, but Becky's face was still there, tears streaming down her cheeks. Sleep couldn't block that. Neither could his dreams. But there was no future for them now. They'd never get over what they'd done to each other.

"Becky," he whispered a moment before the lights went out.

LUKE WOKE UP TO SOMETHING nudging his side. He opened one eye and stared up at Hank.

"What the hell are you doing sleeping in the yard?" Hank asked with his usual finesse.

"Go away," Luke moaned.

"Get your ass up before the folks see you out here."

Luke opened his other eye and saw that it was morning, the dawn light paralyzing to his sensitive eyes. Then he realized something else. His whole body was one big ache. Damn! He didn't think he could move.

"Luke."

Hank's voice reminded him of a bee

buzzing around his head and any minute his stinger was going to sink into him with more pain. Luke forced himself to sit up. He winced, rubbing his shoulder.

"Are you drunk?" The bee buzzed louder.

"No." Luke reached for the redwood chair behind him and used it to pull himself up and into it. He let out a curse word as he did, the pain ripping from his back to his legs.

"What's wrong with you?" Hank persisted, and Luke wished for bug spray.

"I'm in pain, so will you shut up?"

Hank sat in a lawn chair watching him.

A redbird landed on the grass in front of Luke. The bird pecked around, looking for a tasty morsel. He hopped to another spot, his beak reminding Luke of a sewing-machine needle, zinging in and out of the grass with precision swiftness. It crossed his mind that it was probably a female looking for food to feed her babies.

A baby.

God, he'd missed so much of Shane's life.

"Luke, what's wrong with you?"

"Shane is my son." The words came out before he could stop them.

Hank didn't say anything and Luke remembered what Hank had said about Becky finding someone very quickly after Luke had left.

"Did you know?"

Hank shrugged. "I suspected, but the boy has blue eyes."

Luke moved his shoulder around. "I wish you would have told me your suspicions."

"You needed to figure that one out for yourself."

"Thanks, Daddy Dearest."

Hank didn't react to the barb. "How did you find out?"

"Becky told me."

"What happened?"

In a surreal moment, Luke found himself telling his father about yesterday.

"The boy tried to jump the cliffs?"

"Yep. I reached him just in time." He flexed his arm and neck. "But I think I've bruised my shoulder."

"I would suggest having Becky look at it, but I don't suppose that's in the cards."

"No. I can't forgive her for what she's done to me."

"Why not?" was Hank's blunt question.

"Are you joking?"

"No. You may have noticed I don't joke

around. I stopped joking the day I became a father and gave up all rights to my son."

Luke really looked at his father for the first time. "You sound as if that hurt you."

"It did."

"Then why in the hell did you treat me like a second-class citizen?"

"Because I had to."

They were shouting at each other but it seemed like a normal conversation. At least for the Chisums.

"The folks spoiled you, giving you everything you wanted. I had to be the strong one, trying to instill some discipline into your life. You were wild and uncontrollable and I had to put the skids on you. If I hadn't been hard on you, you'd be dead by now. You were always flying off rocks and cliffs, just like Shane. For some reason, you needed to live on the edge of danger, and whether you realize it or not, I'm always at that edge ready to pull you back."

Hearing this from Hank's point of view, Luke was speechless.

"I was the one who pulled you out of that Mustang in the Medina River."

"What?" That hit him like a sucker punch.

"I was in town and heard the buzz and

asked one of the kids what was going on. I hurried out there, but I was too late. The Mustang sailed over just as I drove up. Your friends were all in shock. I dove in but I had hell getting the door open. Luckily the window was down. After a couple of attempts, I was able to undo your seat belt. Your friends were there to help drag you to the bank. The paramedics were waiting."

"I never knew that." A chill ran through him. "When Shane was headed for the cliff and I was too far away to stop him, I kept thinking I was going to watch my kid die and I would never have the chance to hold him or tell him how sorry I was. My next thought was how would I tell Becky."

Luke let out a deep breath, feeling a release talking to Hank. They'd never really talked before. They'd just yelled a lot.

"After I knocked him off the four wheeler, he came up fighting, hitting me with his fists saying how much he hated me. He was alive, though. That was all I could think."

"He must take after you because I've lost track of the number of times you've said that to me."

"You deserved it, though," Luke snapped.

"Maybe," Hank said to Luke's surprise. "I

wanted you to make better choices than me and staying on your ass was the only way I knew how to do that. But it didn't work, did it? You now have a son you don't know."

"And he hates me. He said he doesn't want me for a father."

He could feel Hank's eyes on him. "Doesn't feel very good, does it?"

"No," Luke admitted and looked at his father. "I've never hated you. I just never understood you. I never understood why you had to say such hateful things to me."

"Like what?"

"For one, you said I didn't have what it took to make it in the United States Army."

"Good God, Luke, I was doing everything I could to make you change your mind. After the Mustang crash, I had to tell the folks you were unconscious and I didn't know if you were going to live or die. I vowed then I never wanted to see that look in my mother's eyes again. Going into the army was as high risk as you can get and I tried to dissuade you any way I could. But it didn't work and you chose to fly a damn helicopter and the worry grew. Then the call finally came that I'd dreaded for years." Hank took a breath. "The trip to Walter Reed was the longest of my life."

The silence pulsed with unspoken words, unspoken emotions.

Hank removed his Stetson and studied it. "I'm tired of worrying about you, Luke. And I'm damn tired of feeling guilty. It's time to get your life in order and…"

"Please don't tell me to put my foot in the stirrup and grab the reins."

"Pa gave you that speech, huh?"

"Yep."

Hank stood. "Pa has the right idea. I'm going to be cutting back on my time here at the ranch and it's time for you to take charge."

"You'll never leave this ranch."

"You're wrong." Hank placed his hat on his head. "I only stayed here because of you."

"What?" This was a gut punch he wasn't expecting and it took a moment to catch his breath.

"Whether you believe it or not you've always been my responsibility."

Luke's eyes narrowed. "I don't under-stand."

"I couldn't leave the folks to deal with your shenanigans and when you joined the army I knew that call would come one day. I had to be here. But you're grown now and I'm getting on with my life. I'm moving in with Marla and from now on I'll be sleeping with my wife."

"You stayed here because of me? You gave up your life for me?"

"Yes."

Luke couldn't believe his ears. He'd wondered all these years what kept Hank tied to the ranch. He'd just assumed it was the land and his fight to keep Luke from inheriting it. But it had been because Luke was his son. For a moment he felt sadness for all the wasted years. For the years they could have been father and son.

"And…" Luke watched as Hank grappled for words. His Adam's apple bobbed up and down as if the words were tangled in his throat like barbed wire. "I've never told you, but I'm…I'm proud of you. You not only made it in the army, but you became a hero, risking your own life to save others." The Adam's apple moved convulsively. "I'm sorry I told you like I did. You didn't deserve that."

That was all it took. Luke felt all his anger and resentment fade away. The words meant so much more because he knew they weren't part of Hank's daily vocabulary. Luke stood on shaky legs, eye-to-eye with his father.

"Thank you."

Luke saw something glistening in Hank's eyes. Was that a tear?

Before Luke could look more closely at the phenomenon, Hank grabbed him and hugged him briefly. Hank's thick fingers cut into Luke's aching shoulder, but Luke didn't wince. Nor did he pull away. Miracles didn't happen that often.

Drawing back, Hank said, "Go make this right with Becky."

"I can't."

Hank shrugged. "I'm not going to pressure you. I'm through riding your ass, but you're making a mistake."

Luke ran his hands over his face, the words not pushing his emotional buttons the way they normally would. "Last night when I took Shane home she was waiting in the yard and she was crying. I wanted to say all was forgiven, but I couldn't." He sucked in a breath. "Why can't I do that? Why can't I forgive her?"

Hank patted him on the back. "Because you're a Chisum."

Luke looked squarely at Hank. "I forgive you."

"Then there's hope." Hank nodded toward

the house. "Let's go tell the folks they have a great-grandson."

They fell into step. Suddenly Hank stopped. "Damn, that makes me a grandfather at fifty."

"No, Hank, that makes you a grandfather at around thirty-four or thirty-five."

"Oh, sh—"

They were laughing as they went through the back door. That in itself was a miracle and Luke wondered if there were any miracles left.

Could he forgive Becky?

LUKE HURRIED UPSTAIRS to change out of his filthy clothes and soak his aching body in a hot tub of water. After that, some of the soreness left and he was feeling a whole lot better.

When he walked into the kitchen, everything was quiet and Luke knew Hank had told them. He took his seat, and his mother jumped up and hugged him, and everyone started talking at once.

There were no accusations or harsh words. He thought they accepted the news about Shane rather calmly, and then it hit him. Like Hank, they had suspected all along.

Everyone had suspected, but him.

His mother set a plate of hot waffles in front of him and he channeled his thoughts elsewhere. Sunday was Clover's day off, or that was what she called it, but Luke knew she'd be back in her kitchen by the evening meal.

On Sundays, Hap and Clover went to church and then spent some time at the orphanage. Lucy always fixed Sunday breakfast and it was always waffles.

"You and Becky come to any kind of an agreement?" Pa wanted to know.

"Not yet," Luke replied, digging into the waffles. He realized they'd have to have that conversation and he wasn't looking forward to it.

"Now, Luke…"

"Let him be," Hank intervened. "He'll make his own decisions."

"I want that boy at Great Oaks," Henry said stubbornly.

Luke laid down his fork and wiped his mouth. "He'll come when Becky says he can and not a moment before." He wasn't going to fight Becky over Shane. Right now he didn't have any fight left. And he would never put Shane through anything like that.

"Son…"

"Oh, Luke." Lucy came to the rescue. "Marla and Chelsea are coming to dinner. Isn't that nice? We'll have a family dinner."

"And Shane needs to be here." Henry wouldn't give up and Luke felt the tension building in him again.

Luke pushed away his plate. "In case any of you are interested, the last few days have been rather rough on me. So please give me a break and let me handle my son in my own way."

The doorbell rang, preventing anyone from responding.

Luke shoved back his chair. "I'll get it."

He yanked open the door. Shane stood there. Becky's car was parked out front, but she didn't get out.

"My mother said I had to thank you for saving my life and she said I had to apologize for doing something so—"

"Whoa, kid." Luke held up a hand. "Come back when you want to thank me yourself."

Shane hooked his thumbs in his jeans' pockets and twisted on his sneakers. "Well, you know, it's, like, from me, too."

"It is?"

"Yeah." Shane looked down at his feet. "I was going to come over here and kick your ass for what you did to my mother then I remembered how big you were and I changed my mind. But I also remembered you told me not to jump the cliffs and I thought I'd just show you that you couldn't tell me what to do." He kicked at the concrete with his sneaker. "It was a real dumb idea."

"Real dumb."

"So I'm sorry." Shane looked up then. "And I still want a paint horse."

"Well, why don't we pick one out this morning? Can you stay for a while?"

"I'll ask my mom." He darted to the car and was back in a sec. "She said yes and she'll pick me up later."

"Tell her I'll bring you home. I have to help Hub pull the wheeler out of the river."

"Oh." Shane darted back to the car and it crossed Luke's mind that he should just walk out and talk to Becky himself. But for some reason he didn't.

"That's cool," Shane said, heaving a breath and they walked inside. Luke watched the Tahoe for a second then turned away.

"Mom's meeting some friends and they're

planning a baby shower for Annie. You should see Annie. She looks like she swallowed a basketball. I tease her…" Shane stopped talking as three pairs of eyes stared at him.

"Why are they staring at me?" he whispered to Luke.

"I told them about you," Luke whispered back.

"Ooooh."

Lucy couldn't stand it any longer. She ran to Shane and hugged him, cupping his face. "You're so beautiful."

Shane frowned. "I'm a boy, Mrs. Lucy. I'm not beautiful."

"You are to me. How about some breakfast? We have waffles."

"No, thank you. I already had… You got waffles?"

"Yes. Have a seat. I'll fix you a plate."

Luke sat and watched his son devour a stack of waffles. He didn't show any signs of nervousness. Shane was a social person. He'd fit in anywhere.

"Shane and I are going to look at the paints," Luke said, getting to his feet. "I promised him one."

"I'm coming," Henry said.

Shane jumped up and handed Henry his cane.

"Thanks, boy."

"You're welcome, Mr. Henry."

They all got into Luke's pickup, even Hank. At the corral, Shane climbed the pipe fence to get a better view of the horses munching on grass. Some frolicked in the morning breeze.

Shane pointed to a brown-and-white paint, snorting and throwing up his head. "I like him."

"Nah," Henry said. "He's still got too much fire in him."

"But I can ride real good, Mr. Henry."

Luke knew better than to step in and say he couldn't have the horse. Shane would only want it that much more.

Hank pointed to a black-and-white gelding. "Look at the flanks on that one, Shane. He'll run like the wind."

"What's his name?"

"Choctaw."

"Choctaw." Shane repeated it. "Yep. That's my horse. When can I take him home?"

A pregnant pause followed the question.

"The horse stays here," Luke said.

"Jeez." Shane jumped off the fence. "I knew there'd be conditions."

"Don't you want to come here?" Hank asked.

"I suppose," Shane muttered.

"You don't have to come here if you don't want to," Luke told him.

"It's not that." Shane hooked his thumbs into his jeans again.

"What is it then?" Luke asked.

Shane looked at him. "It feels kind of strange, you know."

"It feels strange to me, too, Shane."

"Oh."

"So we'll just take it slow, okay?"

"Okay." Shane climbed back onto the fence. "Will Choctaw come to me?"

"Sure." Luke climbed up beside his son and whistled. Several horses reared their heads and trotted to the fence, Choctaw in the lead.

Shane held out his hand to the horse and four generations of Chisum men held their breath as they realized a bond was forming in a way they'd never thought possible.

CHAPTER NINETEEN

THE DAYS FELL INTO a pattern. After school, Hub would drop Shane off at the ranch and Becky picked him up on her way home. She never got out. She'd honk and Shane would shout "Bye," then run out to her. Luke was left standing at the door, watching them drive away. But still he made no effort to talk to Becky. They both seemed to need it that way.

Lucy wasn't constantly calling Becky to come over. Lucy depended on Becky for medical advice and Luke didn't want to stand in the way of that. His mother seemed fine, though, and so was Henry.

It was now Shane's job to drive Henry around in the Ranger, and he did it as if he'd been doing it all his life. Shane was very careful helping Henry and telling him to watch his step. Henry thrived on the attention and so did Shane.

Luke's favorite time was the time he spent alone with his son. He taught him how to handle Choctaw and beamed like a proud daddy when Shane caught on quickly. His absolute favorite thing was when Shane talked about his childhood, the gifts he'd gotten for Christmases, the birthday parties Becky had thrown, a dog that had died and he was still sad about and his love of trucks. Shane loved to talk and Luke never tired of listening to him.

Hank had moved to San Antonio to live with Marla, but he was at the ranch every morning and had breakfast with them. He worked every day like always, but some days he quit early and went home to Marla. Luke took up the slack, stepping into Hank's boots. It was expected of him and this time, he expected it of himself.

He had a kid to think about.

The auction came and the weekend was busy. Hank hired Shane to work the gates and Luke thought he paid him too much. But Luke didn't say anything. That Monday, Luke took the money and opened Shane a bank account. He made a deal with his son. He would match everything Shane put into the account. Shane could hardly contain his excitement. When his birthday arrived, he'd be able to buy a monster truck, as he put it.

Luke intended to be there for that birthday.

He'd missed so many, but he couldn't let himself think about that.

He couldn't let himself think about Becky, either.

THEN THE DAY CAME when Shane said he couldn't come to the ranch. He had to visit his dad in San Antonio. Luke should have known it was coming, but it struck him with the power of a Nolan Ryan fastball, smack in the center of his heart.

Danny wasn't Shane's father.

Not wanting to cause problems, Luke didn't say anything. But that Monday, he drove into San Antonio to see Danny. He wasn't sure what he was going to say, but he knew they had to talk.

Danny's accounting firm was located in a business park. He hadn't called ahead, but Danny saw him right away. Luke walked into his office and took in the leather chairs, mahogany desk and filing cabinets amid electronic equipment. He also noticed the photos on the wall: a blond boy and girl, a woman and Shane when he was about ten.

Luke wanted to snatch the picture down, but he maintained his composure.

"Luke." Danny rose to his feet.

As before, he thought Danny looked much the same as he had in high school, thin with wire-rimmed glasses and a nervous smile, except now he had less hair.

Luke had come here for a reason, but for the life of him he had a hard time vocalizing that reason. "I'm not sure why I'm here," he admitted.

"Is it about Shane?"

"Yes," Luke replied. "I'd like to thank you for being there for him all these years."

"You're welcome. It was a pleasure." Danny's eyes narrowed. "Isn't Becky the real reason you're here, though?"

"No."

"You're lying, Luke. It's killing you that she married me."

And there it was—the crux of his problem. She'd married Danny. He tried to shake it off, but the truth had him by the throat and wouldn't let go.

"When she found out you were gone, she cried for a solid week. I told her that wasn't good for her or the baby and she had to pull herself together. But she was scared to death, scared of Hub, scared of being a single mom. I was crazy about Becky so I said let's just get married. And we did. But Becky still cried at night and I wanted to kill you for what you'd done to her."

Luke's tongue felt heavy, but he managed to say, "I thought she loved you."

"Becky and I love each other but we weren't in love. That was the problem. She could never love me the way she loved you. When she made the decision to leave, I was hurt, but she did me a favor. I found the real thing." He glanced at the photo of the woman on the wall. "I'm happy now. I just wish Becky was."

"I've got to go." Luke turned toward the door. He'd heard enough.

"Luke."

He paused in his stride.

"Don't be a macho male and screw this up. Do what you should have done sixteen years ago."

Luke walked away with those words ringing in his ears. He didn't have the urge to run. He wasn't running anymore. From somewhere deep within him, he had to find the courage to forgive.

And he prayed it wasn't too late.

WEDNESDAY NIGHT was Annie's baby shower. Becky stacked finger sandwiches neatly on a tray and set a fruit plate out along with veggies and ranch dip. Then she arranged a spring bouquet of flowers for the table.

"Let me do that," Rachel said.

"Gladly. I'm hopeless at decorating."

"Oh, please." Rachel sighed.

Molly carried a large punch bowl filled with pink sangria and carefully set it down. Tessa followed with a cake.

"Everything is so lovely," June said, eyeing the table. June had wanted to have the shower at her house, so they did.

Annie waddled from the kitchen, munching on a sandwich. "Sorry. I was hungry." She stared at the gifts piled high on the coffee table. "Everything is so nice. Thanks. You're such wonderful friends." Tears gathered in her eyes.

Becky took her arm. "Come and sit. And no tears."

"I cry over everything and most of the time they're happy tears." Annie eased onto the sofa.

Zoë's cry stopped the conversation.

"I'll get her," Becky said and lifted the

baby out of the Pack 'n Play. She was so soft, so sweet, and Becky thought about Shane at that age. And everything that Luke had missed. Now she had to fight tears.

Tessa snapped several pictures and then asked, "May I hold her?" Becky handed off Zoë, who was now quiet and enjoying the attention.

"She's adorable," Tessa said, sitting and holding Zoë with a look of wonder on her face.

June watched her future daughter-in-law. "Have you and Cole thought of setting a wedding date?"

Without taking her eyes off the baby, Tessa replied, "Cole said if his sister or his mother asked that question I was to say…"

"Never mind," June said. "I can imagine the rest."

They laughed.

"I'm not sure why Cole included me, because I've only asked about ten times." Annie kept a straight face.

They laughed again.

Molly sank down by Tessa's chair to play with Zoë, tickling her stomach.

"Where's Sammy tonight?" Tessa asked.

"With Marshall. I told him two pieces of

candy was all Sammy was allowed, but Marshall never listens to me." Molly rolled her eyes. "Sammy will be so hyper when Brady and I get home that we'll have to peel him off the ceiling. I'm going to have to have a talk with my future father-in-law."

Molly clamped a hand over her mouth as she realized what she'd said. "That slipped out. And before anyone asks, we're not engaged, but we're thinking maybe before Thanksgiving. We'd like to be a family for the holidays."

"That's nice," June said, staring pointedly at Tessa, who chose to ignore her future mother-in-law.

Rachel lifted Zoë into her arms. "I'll give her a bottle. She's ready to go night-night." She kissed the baby's rosy cheek.

While Rachel fed Zoë, Becky and Tessa moved the Pack 'n Play into a bedroom. Rachel laid her daughter inside, stroking her hair for a minute. "She's out like a light." They walked back into the living room.

"How's the house coming?" Annie asked Rachel.

"Great, but sometimes I think it's too slow. When it's finished, we plan to move in as a family. I'm so excited. Who would have ever thought that I would have to come back to River Bluff to find true happiness?"

"Happiness! I've forgotten what it feels like." Becky hadn't even realized she'd spoken the words out loud until she noticed everyone was staring at her.

She frowned. "Did that sound really sad?"

"Yes," Annie said, watching her with concerned eyes.

"I'm sorry. Luke is not speaking to me, but he and Shane are getting along like a house on fire. I'm grateful for that, but I wonder if happiness is in the cards for me."

"Becky…"

The doorbell rang and Becky hurried to answer it, glad for the reprieve. Autumn, Tessa's mother, arrived with Sunny and Joey, Tessa's sister and little nephew. Joey ran to Tessa and she picked him up, holding him close. He stared bright-eyed at all the gifts and they knew who would be helping to open them.

The bell pealed again and Becky opened the door to Sarah Diamonte, Rachel's mother. She was followed by Sally, Bobbie Sue and Steffi. Soon the living room was full of River Bluff women.

Angela Carrick and Lucy came together.

Lucy hugged Becky tightly and Becky saw all the worry in her eyes. Tonight wasn't the time for a talk though. But Becky couldn't keep her thoughts from straying to Luke.

She'd been waiting for some sign from him and she was still waiting. He wasn't ever going to forgive her. He was a Chisum and Chisums didn't forgive.

Bull.

Some day soon she might have to tell him what she thought about that.

THE POKER GAME was in full swing but Luke was having a hard time concentrating. He thought about Danny and all that he'd said, and guilt weighed heavily upon him. When those thoughts grew painful, he thought about Shane. He'd like to take him to San Antonio for the weekend to look at trucks and to see a Spurs game.

But he'd have to ask Becky. He wasn't ready to do that.

A chip suddenly hit his chest and bounced onto the floor. He glanced up to see Brady glaring at him.

"What?"

"It's your turn to bet or do something,"

Brady told him. "We've been waiting for five minutes."

Luke couldn't even remember what he had under his dog tags. "I'm out," he said and stood.

"You're out for the night?" Cole asked with a note of concern in his voice.

"Yep. I'm not in a mood for poker."

"Hot damn," Jake said. "We need to write this date on a wall somewhere—the day Luke didn't want to play poker."

"No one's writing anything on these newly painted walls," Cole said. The game was at Cole's tonight and he was watching everyone like a hawk in his and Tessa's recently completed home.

"I'll catch you guys next week." Luke headed for the door.

"Luke."

He looked back at Brady and saw all their worried expressions. Even ol' Knut had an anxious demeanor.

"I'm fine. I just have some decisions to make."

WHEN BECKY ARRIVED HOME, the only light shining was the one over the kitchen sink—the one her father always left on when she was out. She leaned against her car and breathed in the fresh night air slightly tinged with the scent of the hibiscus bushes blooming against the house.

She ran her hands up her arms, feeling restless and on edge. Sleep would not come easily tonight. She glanced up at the dark expanse of sky and wished she could get lost in its vastness, feel its power and magnificence.

Would that make her happy? Suddenly she knew what the restlessness was all about. She wanted to be happy again. She wanted to laugh, dance and be held in the arms of a man she loved. That might not be within her reach.

But she knew a place that had brought her only happiness.

And she needed to feel that happiness tonight.

LUKE DROVE TO THE CORRALS. He was sure the folks were in bed and he wasn't ready to call it a night. He was feeling things he couldn't explain—loneliness, yet he was around people all the time. But a part of him, a vital part, was empty and incomplete. Even his son couldn't fill that void.

He told himself it was the secrets. They'd taken him down as far as he'd ever been, but he'd found his way back. Life was good. Life was better.

And he was lying.

Just as Danny had said.

Becky was the reason for the loneliness. And until he came to terms with his feelings for her, he was always going to be lonely.

He whistled and Cochise appeared out of the darkness. There was only one way to get rid of the knot in his gut.

To saddle up and ride.

BECKY HEARD THE THUNDER of hooves before she saw the rider. She'd walked to the pond on the Circle C where she and Luke had spent a lot of happy evenings. As a teenager, she'd made the trek many times, and Luke had always been waiting for her. Tonight she was out here alone. She took a deep breath, realizing the rider could be anyone.

She would be very quiet and the person wouldn't even know she was there. The evening breeze felt damp against her skin. The moonlight played with the water, creating eerie dancing shadows and bathing the landscape in an iridescent haze. But it was soothing in a way—until her space had been invaded.

A creak of a saddle and then footsteps. The person was walking straight to where she was sitting. She braced herself against the oak tree, feeling the jagged bark pressing into her back. Her hands were clammy and her breath came in short gasps as she waited.

A man emerged in the moonlight, tall and erect. And familiar. She didn't have to see his face to know it was Luke. The fear inside her was replaced with another. But there was no way to avoid him now. They had to face each other.

And the past.

Luke stopped for a moment to look at the pond and its shadowy reflection. His boots crunched on the grass as he moved closer. Then he suddenly stopped and she knew he sensed he wasn't alone. A couple more steps and he was within three feet of her.

"Becky?" There was puzzlement in his voice.

"Yes." She cleared her throat. "It's me."

He stood there for a full minute without saying a word. Fear tugged at her heart—a heart that was already broken. His silence was tearing her apart and she had to leave.

"I'm sorry. I'm trespassing. I'll go."

"No," he said abruptly, and something scurried in the underbrush and then they heard a splash in the water. Neither paid any attention to whatever it was. "We need to talk."

She settled against the tree. "Okay."

He sank to the ground. "How did you get here?" His voice had a rough edge, but she could still hear the underlying softness, and she wanted to reach out, touch him and melt herself into him. It wasn't the sky that held her captive. It was Luke. It had always been Luke.

"I walked," she managed to say.

"Why?"

"I was feeling a little down," she admitted before she could stop herself.

He was immediately alert. "Is it about Shane? Is he okay?"

She drew up her knees. "Shane is fine. I worried how the truth was going to affect him, but he's done very well. He loves the Circle C and your family."

"Why wouldn't he? That's where he should have been from the start."

She gripped her hands as she felt the shadows of the past creep along her skin. "I wish I could change what happened, but I can't. At the time, I did what I thought I had to. I was too young and insecure to do anything else."

Please forgive me. But she didn't say the words. She couldn't force the words from him.

"I spoke to Danny."

That surprised her. "You did?"

"Yes. He said you never loved him the way you loved me."

"That's true."

"Then why couldn't we trust in that love? Why couldn't it help us make better decisions? Why wasn't it strong enough to make us see that it was all that mattered?"

"Because we were too young," she replied.

"Yes, and yet, we keep coming back to this place where we felt that love."

There was silence for a moment—an unbearable silence.

Luke spoke first. "Why do we still keep hurting each other?"

"I guess because some things are unforgivable." She felt a catch in her throat and knew she had to get away before she burst into tears.

He isn't ever going to forgive me.

She stood on shaky legs, the night air now feeling chilly to her heated nerves. "I'd better get back."

As she walked by him, Luke knew if he let her go, his life would be as empty and black as the nightmares that haunted him. In that moment, he knew he had made lousy choices in the past, but this time he had to get it right.

He caught her hand and linked his fingers with hers. He felt strength in the long fingers curled around his. And she was strong, making a life as a single mom. Making a life for their son.

Without him.

And that was the problem—the one thing that was tearing him up. He hadn't been there for them.

He pulled her down into his lap and felt her tears against his face.

"You have to forgive me, Luke. You have to forgive me." Her broken cries ripped through him like a chain saw.

"Shh." He wiped away her tears.

"Luke…"

"Shh," he said again.

She stilled and rested her head on his shoulder.

He drew a deep breath. "There's nothing to forgive."

"You mean that?" She raised her head to look into his eyes.

"Yes. I really love you, Becky, and when you love someone that much, the pain and the pleasure is that much more intense. And forgiveness is a given."

"Oh, Luke. I love you." Her shaky hand stroked his face.

"I think we had to come back to this place to remember that."

She kissed his cheek, his nose, and he took her lips in a slow, heated caress of total forgiveness.

He tasted the salt of her tears and he tasted the love that had always been there. Resting his forehead against hers, he said, "I've just had a hard time forgiving myself. I let you down. I let Shane down. And yet, you still love me."

"Yes." She kissed him behind his ear and her lips traveled to his neck.

"Let's never keep anything from each other again," he groaned, running his fingers through her hair.

"Never," she murmured, an ache in her voice.

"Let's get married as soon as we can, like we should have sixteen years ago."

"Okay." Tears rolled from her eyes and Luke kissed them away.

"Don't cry, Bec."

"I can't help it." She hiccuped. "I'm so happy."

He kissed her wet lips. "We'll build a house overlooking this pond so we'll never forget how much we love each other."

"I'd like that." A smile chased away the tears—a Becky smile. Luke knew they were going to make it.

He slowly undid the buttons on her blouse and bore her down on the grass. "Do you think we're ever going to make love in a bed?"

"I sincerely hope so." She giggled, and Luke felt at peace and at home for the first time.

EPILOGUE

IT WAS JUNE.

A time for weddings.

To Becky, the whirl of the helicopter blades sounded as enchanting as the wedding march. Luke was here. They were getting married today.

Rachel adjusted the baby's breath in Becky's hair and smiled at her in the mirror. "You look happy."

"I am." Becky smiled back.

Molly came into the room with an empty box. "The guys all have boutonnieres," she said. "I have Luke's and Shane's left, but I just heard the helicopter, so I'll go down in a minute and pin them on."

"I snapped pictures of all our handsome guys, and of course, some guests." Tessa held up her camera. "And I plan to get more later."

"Thank you," Becky said.

"Will someone help me, please?" Annie begged, floundering in a chair like an upside-down beetle.

Tessa and Molly ran to pull her up. "God, I've gained fifty pounds," Annie groaned, and then beamed a smile. "But I don't care. I love every minute of this."

Becky turned in her chair. "You look beautiful."

"Speaking of beautiful." Annie leaned over and hugged her. "You look gorgeous in that dress."

Becky wore a strapless off-white dress with a fitted bodice and a skirt that flared around her ankles. A white satin ribbon nestled around her waist and trailed down the back of her skirt.

She pulled up the top. "I don't know why I let y'all talk me into this dress. It's too revealing." She adjusted the bodice again.

"Stop that," Annie said. "You have nice breasts so show them off. It's not like they're going to fall out or anything."

Becky looked down at her cleavage. "I didn't have much in high school, but after Shane was born, I seemed to—" she cupped her hands in front of herself "—blossom."

Annie looked down at her bulging breasts. "Oh, please, tell me these aren't going to stay like this."

"They don't," Rachel said with a smile.

"We talk about the weirdest things." Molly shook her head.

Becky looked around at the newly decorated upstairs room at the Wild Card Saloon. "I can't believe I'm getting married in a bar."

Rachel placed her hands on her hips. "And what's wrong with this tastefully decorated bar?"

"Absolutely nothing. I'd marry Luke in a funeral home."

They burst out laughing.

"I'm going to spend the rest of my life loving him and every tomorrow is going to be filled with that much more love."

Molly looked thoughtful. "I think that's a country song."

Becky smiled at her friends, feeling the love and happiness in the room.

LUKE CIRCLED the Wild Card looking for the spot Jake had designated for him to land.

"When can I fly the chopper?" his copilot asked.

"When you've had training and get your license."

"Ah, man, you gonna be that kind of dad?"

"You bet."

"Look." Shane pointed below. "There's Hank, Marla and Chelsea. And Grandpa. He has on the starched white shirt that he hates." Shane waved madly.

"Doubt if they can see you."

"I don't care. I see them. Oh, look, there are Danny and Noreen." The kid shifted gears faster than a formula one race-car driver.

Shane looked at him. "I don't call him *Dad* anymore."

Something that felt like warm honey slid down Luke's throat. "You can if you want to."

"Nah. I'm your kid, right?"

"Right."

"And Danny said he's cool with it."

Luke lifted an eyebrow. "He's cool with it?"

"Okay, he didn't say *cool,* but that's what

he meant." Shane straightened his jacket. "Mom's going to be so freaked when she sees us in these tuxedo jackets."

Luke was freaked already. The past couple of weeks had been a whirlwind, and this day couldn't get here fast enough. He and Becky had talked about where to have the wedding. They wanted a neutral place and they wanted it simple. Jake had said the Wild Card was finished, and they could have the grand opening and the wedding all at the same time. The idea had sounded great to them.

"Jake's waving," Shane said.

"Hold tight, kid. We're going down." And those words had never sounded so good. Below, everything he wanted waited.

Becky was there.

WHEN LUKE SAW BECKY in the white dress, the years rolled away and he was looking at the Becky he'd fallen in love with—sweet Rebecca Lynn. His hand shook as he took her hand and they said their vows, surrounded by their friends and family. It was simple. It was perfect.

They shared a long kiss. The guys whistled and hollered.

The minister held up a hand. "I present to you Mr. and Mrs. Luke Chisum. And their son, Shane."

"And now, ladies and gentlemen…" Jake's voice rose above the applause. He walked outside to the porch railing and broke a beer bottle over the new wood. "I declare the Wild Card Saloon officially open for business. Let's party and play poker. Food and drinks courtesy of the Chisums."

"OhmyGod!" Annie's voice stopped the cheering.

Becky followed Annie's gaze and saw the puddle at Annie's feet. "My water broke," she wailed.

Becky hurried to her and helped her into a chair. Blake seemed turned to stone.

"Call the doctor," Becky said to Blake.

"Oh. Oh. Yes." Blake frantically searched his pockets for a phone. "I'm sorry. I'm just so nervous."

Cole came to his rescue and handed him a cell phone.

"Becky," Annie said between deep breaths. "The baby's early. It's too early."

"Sometimes babies are early. Do your breathing. Everything's going to be fine."

"No. It isn't. I've ruined your wedding day." Annie burst into tears.

"You've ruined nothing."

"The doctor said to get her to the emergency room in San Antonio. She's meeting us there." Blake kissed his wife's cheek. "Hang on, honey. We'll be there in no time."

"You bet we will," Luke said. "The copter's outside."

Within minutes, the guys had Annie loaded. Rachel brought pillows and blankets to make her comfortable.

Before boarding, Luke glanced back to see Shane looking lost. Luke rushed back to him. "Son, take care of our guests and make sure everyone has a good time. I'll call you."

Suddenly Shane gripped him around the waist. "I will, Dad."

Luke held his son for a moment longer and then hurried to the helicopter, with a clogged throat and wet eyes.

As he slid into his seat, his eyes caught

Becky's. She was kneeling beside Annie and Blake. Luke winked and Becky smiled.

"Ready?" he asked at the controls.

"Ready," Becky replied, her eyes shining as brightly as any stars he'd ever seen.

As the copter hovered off the ground, Luke saw Cole, Tessa and June, Jake and Rachel and Brady and Molly running for their cars.

The flight was smooth and easy, and soon they landed in San Antonio. The emergency crew was waiting and wheeled Annie away with Blake following.

"I have to move the chopper," Luke shouted to Becky. "I'll catch you inside."

Becky blew him a kiss and hurried after the stretcher.

Luke had to do a little finagling with a parking-garage attendant, but he found a spot to leave the helicopter.

When he went inside the hospital, the gang and June had arrived. He kissed Becky. "How's it going?"

"They've taken her into delivery. The baby's coming."

They sat waiting. Not much was said.

Brady pulled out a twenty. "I bet it's a boy. Any takers?"

"Sure," Jake said, reaching for his wallet. "I'll raise your bet. It's a girl."

"I'm in," Cole said, digging in his pocket.

"Will you guys stop," Becky said. "This is not poker. We're having a baby." She walked off down the hall to check on Annie and Blake.

Luke watched her walk away, still in her wedding dress, and he thought she'd never looked more beautiful. In a moment, she came rushing back, her cheeks flushed.

"The baby has arrived. Elizabeth June Smith weighed in at five pounds and seven ounces. Everyone is fine, even Blake. He's already calling her Libby."

"Oh, my." June held a hand to her chest. "They named the baby June."

"Now the waterworks," Cole teased.

Everyone hugged and couldn't seem to stop smiling.

"I have to see my granddaughter." June wiped at her eyes.

Finally Cole himself brushed away a tear and grabbed Tessa's hand. "We're going to see our niece."

"And I have to take pictures." Tessa reached for her camera. The three of them hurried down the hall.

Luke reached for his cell and called Shane, needing to let his son know everything was okay.

After he clicked off, he said, "He's telling everyone. There was a lot of shouting in the background. After they finish eating, they're setting up the tables for a night of poker."

"Hot damn." Brady grinned. "We'll be back in time for that."

Jake slapped Luke on the back. "Go, for heaven's sakes. Go have a honeymoon."

Brady gave them a push. "Go. It's about sixteen years overdue."

"Wait," Rachel said, straightening the baby's breath in Becky's hair, and then she slipped back into Jake's arms.

"Just a sec," Molly called, and quickly retied the ribbon around Becky's waist that had come undone.

"Now that's just a waste of time, honey. Luke is just going to undo it."

"Behave," Molly said to Brady as his arms went around her.

"Go," Jake urged.

Luke took Becky's hand and they walked out of the hospital. Outside in the moonlight, he took her in his arms. "Mrs. Chisum, how would you like to make love in a bed tonight?"

"Why, Mr. Chisum, that would be lovely."

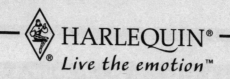

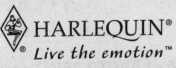

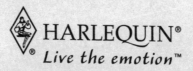

HARLEQUIN®
INTRIGUE®

BREATHTAKING ROMANTIC SUSPENSE

Shared dangers and passions lead to electrifying
romance and heart-stopping suspense!

Every month, you'll meet six new heroes
who are guaranteed to make your spine tingle
and your pulse pound. With them you'll enter
into the exciting world of Harlequin Intrigue—
where your life is on the line
and so is your heart!

THAT'S INTRIGUE—
ROMANTIC SUSPENSE
AT ITS BEST!

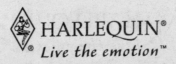

HARLEQUIN®
Live the emotion™

Harlequin® Historical
Historical Romantic Adventure!

*Imagine a time of chivalrous
knights and unconventional ladies,
roguish rakes and impetuous
heiresses, rugged cowboys
and spirited frontierswomen—
these rich and vivid tales will
capture your imagination!*

*Harlequin Historical . . .
they're too good to miss!*

HHDIR06

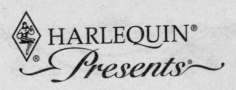

HARLEQUIN®
Presents~

**The world's bestselling romance series...
The series that brings you your favorite authors,
month after month:**

Helen Bianchin...Emma Darcy
Lynne Graham...Penny Jordan
Miranda Lee...Sandra Marton
Anne Mather...Carole Mortimer
Susan Napier...Michelle Reid

and many more uniquely talented authors!

Wealthy, powerful, gorgeous men...
Women who have feelings just like your own...
The stories you love, set in exotic, glamorous locations...

HARLEQUIN®
Presents~

Seduction and Passion Guaranteed!

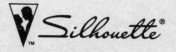